"READY YOUR CARBINES."

They hadn't gone more than a couple steps before Donovan could see over the grass-fuzzed crest. There were Indians down there, all right. Six, eight, maybe a dozen of them.

It wasn't some wagon train or isolated homestead they were shooting at though. It was a small herd of buffalo.

Or more accurately there had been a herd there. The buffalo were on the run now, a band of perhaps a hundred of them disappearing toward the west under a yellow cloud of dust.

Immediately below the patrol, the Indians were dismounted in the midst of their kill from that herd. Four . . . no, five . . . dead or dying buffs lay in the grass. The Indians had no idea they weren't alone out here. They were off their horses and gathered together in a bunch, talking to each other and gesturing, no doubt recounting their prowess and accuracy in bringing the buffalo down.

It wasn't a war party, thank goodness, Donovan realized. Just a bunch of wild Indians collecting meat for the pot.

"At the trot now."

The uneasiness in Donovan's belly disappeared.

"At the gallop."

"Oh, Jesus!" Donovan blurted, and the fluttering fear returned stronger than ever.

"Charge!"

TROOPER DONOVAN

FRANK RODERUS

LEISURE BOOKS NEW YORK CITY

For Dave and Ludmila

A LEISURE BOOK®

June 2000

Published by

Dorchester Publishing Co., Inc.
276 Fifth Avenue
New York, NY 10001

ISBN 0-8439-4731-4

TROOPER DONOVAN

Chapter One

It wasn't much of a post. But then, it wasn't much of an outfit, either. Both were brand new and green as grass. Neither had any history behind it. No triumphs, no glory, no campaign ribbons to show off with pride.

That was just fine by John Donovan. All he wanted was to do his duty, draw his pay, and be left the hell alone. If there was glory to be had, some other guy was welcome to it.

Donovan climbed down from the back of the freight wagon that had transported him and thirteen other recruits out from Leavenworth—fourteen all told, so it wasn't an unlucky number—and reached back inside for the canvas kit bag that held the sum total of all his worldly possessions.

He was achingly conscious of the sight he and the others presented. Or itchingly aware, which in truth might be the better way to put it. The ill-fitting woolen uniforms itched something awful in the heat of the early summer.

The yellow stripe on the light blue undress trouser was bold and clear. Later on, the stripes would fade and turn pale, but that would take days and miles and many washings. Later on, the gray flannel shirts would soften and the dark blue shell jacket take on an unkempt, baggy sort of comfort.

And later on, they should all be so lucky, maybe even the unregenerate sons of cobblers' benches would yield a semblance of comfort from the stiff and awkward highleg boots.

But all of that would be later on, or so one would hope. None of it was now.

Recruit John Donovan—no, now it was *Trooper* Donovan, if you please—stamped his feet, arched his back, and sought to get some feeling back into limbs numbed by days of travel perched atop boxes, barrels, and bales of goods all destined, as were he and his fellow troopers, for Camp Horan, Kansas, and N Troop of the recently formed and yet to be tested Seventh United States Cavalry.

With any sort of luck, John Donovan hoped, he would serve out his enlistment in peace and harmony, with little to do but tend the post vegetable garden, groom the officers' horses, and answer the occasional call to assembly.

With any sort of luck.

Chapter Two

"Is *every*thing in this outfit leftover old issue?" Donovan grumbled. He was perched on an empty packing crate that served as chair, stool, and dining table. The crate and three others like it were placed near the cavelike entrance to the sod-roofed dugout that served Donovan's four in lieu of proper barracks. At the moment he was inspecting the saddle issued to him. Surely there had to be at least one available from quartermaster stores in better repair than this.

The seat leather was dry, and the wood of the tree was exposed underneath. It, too, showed cracks caused by age and drying. He scraped at a suspicious-looking stain with the nail of his right thumb and was rewarded with flakes of some ancient, brown-black substance. He rather hoped it was only manure. The only other likely culprit would be blood, and while John Donovan was not a particularly superstitious man, he would just as soon not be sitting a dead man's saddle, thank you very much.

Another member of Donovan's four overheard and commented, "Hell, man, even most of us are leftovers from the war. You think that saddle is bad? They're still issuing bacon and hardtack dated from '64. Says so right on the boxes." The man—Donovan thought his name was Sims—added, "The War Department is getting so cheap, they tell me they're gonna start policing the latrine sinks and reissuing bacon if they find any chunks big enough."

Donovan grunted. And smiled just a little.

He felt ill at ease and far from being settled into the new quarters. Not that there was much to them.

No one knew if Camp Horan would be made a permanent post along the Smoky Hill route to Colorado and the gold diggings, and little had been done to provide for the comfort of man or horse.

The officers lived in relative ease in conical Sibley tents, usually with flooring made from sacking or even real carpet. The enlisted men were quartered in dugouts, shallow depressions carved out of hillsides and roofed with saplings and sod. Rather than waste the large timbers that would be needed to produce platoon- or even squad-size accommodation, the dugouts were made only large enough to contain four men, the most basic unit in a cavalry command. These four men worked, slept and when necessary fought together. In battle one of the men normally held all four horses in the rear while the other three were free to advance on foot.

Four men, obviously, comprised a four. Three fours made a squad, two squads made a platoon, and two platoons formed a troop. N Troop had been seriously undermanned before Donovan and the others in his draft of replacements arrived.

Still were, actually. Regulation called for sixty men to

the troop, but apparently no one expected that paper figure to be met in practice. And the outfit continued to be seriously shortchanged, as well, when it came to any of them knowing what the army required of them, Donovan realized. Virtually no training had been given to them thus far, and what little had been was mostly in the way of lectures and loud cursing.

So far the new men had uniforms—such as they were—and now saddles, sabers, and assorted other accoutrements. Perhaps tomorrow they would draw carbines and revolvers and horses.

Or then again, perhaps not. The good thing was that it wasn't his worry. Whatever happened, it was not Donovan's to worry about. All he had to do was keep his eyes down and his mouth shut. And do whatever anyone told him to do.

It was a relief to think about that, and he reminded himself of it often.

"You a leftover too, Donovan?" Sims asked.

Donovan shook his head. "You?"

The private nodded. "Wounded twice. Once at Malvern Hill and once, dagnabbit, the last dang morning of the scrape, out along the road to Appomattox."

"Kill you, did they?"

"Sure did. Twice. Didn't I mention that part?" Sims grinned.

"Any particular army?" Donovan asked.

Sims's expression became serious again. "Two things you don't want to ask in this man's army nowadays, Donovan. One is what his name was back in the States. The other is what side he fought on. Of course, you do whatever you like. It's just friendly advice."

Donovan nodded. "I'll keep both those things in mind. Thanks."

Frank Roderus

"You'll be all right, soldier. Just watch what I do." Sims's grin returned. "Then do the opposite."

Donovan laughed and began rubbing soap into the brittle leather of his new broken-down saddle. It badly needed cleaning and then oiling. But it would be all right.

Everything would.

Chapter Three

Donovan tilted his head. Squinted. Walked around to the other side of the horse and tried looking from another angle. "Nope," he said aloud. "It doesn't get any better no matter how I look at it." He sighed. "Another damned leftover from the war."

This awkward and ungainly-looking creature now belonged to Donovan, and he to it. It was a relationship that would continue until one of them was dead or crippled, and this was not a fine, fair foot to start out on. The horse was—there was no charitable way to put it—the animal was just plain butt-ugly. A long, curving scar marred the left side of its face, and half its ear on that side was missing as well. Its coat was patchy and mottled as if with disease, and it stood hipshot and head down, as if it hadn't strength enough to stand full upright and aware. It did not look like much of a mount. But it belonged to Donovan now, and he belonged to it.

Ed Sims and the other two men in the four—Louie

Gordon, and the other called himself John Smith—only grinned at the new recruit's discomfort.

They, Donovan had learned, were old-timers in the Seventh. They'd enlisted all of three months back.

"Stand back here and clap your hands," Smith suggested.

"Why?"

Smith's grin got wider, but he did not explain.

With a shrug Donovan walked around to the back end of the horse, far enough away that it could not easily reach him if it decided to kick, and clapped his hands sharply together. The brown horse did not so much as twitch its one good ear.

"Go ahead," Smith said. "Yell. Stamp your feet. Make some noise."

Donovan looked at him, then at the horse. Realization dawned. "Damn thing's deaf, isn't it?"

"As a post," Smith agreed.

"A lot of the older horses are like that," Gordon put in. "During the war the Remount Service was in a hurry to get horses bought and delivered. It was quicker and easier to break a horse's eardrums and make it deaf than to teach the thing not to bolt at the sound of cannon and musketry. Took weeks off the training, they tell me. We still get a lot of horses they done that to."

"That's cruel," Donovan said.

"Sure it is," Gordon agreed. "But it worked. That's all the army cared about. It still is."

"Look at it this way," Sims said. "At least you won't have to worry about your horse getting crazy and running away with you into a bunch of wild Indians. This critter has likely seen about everything there is to see. It should be steady under you, else it'd already be dead. Whatever cavalryman used to have it woulda killed it himself if he couldn't trust it in a scrap."

"Unless the horse really is crazy and got him killed first," Smith said with a wink.

"Aren't you the cheerful one," Donovan told him, which brought another grin from Smith.

"What the hell are you people standing around jawing about?" the squad corporal roared from the far end of the picket line. "Nobody eats until morning stables are done. Now, get busy."

Donovan picked up his newly issued dandybrush and cautiously approached the aging warhorse, careful to step far enough out to the side that the horse could see him coming and wouldn't likely be startled by his touch.

Chapter Four

"When do we get to sight these in?" Donovan asked. He was seated on an empty hardtack crate outside the mouth of their dugout with a stubby and hard-used but reasonably clean and rust-free Spencer carbine in his lap.

"We don't," Sims told him.

"How can you fight with a gun if you don't even know where it shoots?" he asked.

"Don't worry about it," Gordon said. "If you're shooting from horseback you can't hold steady enough to take aim, and if you dismount to fight as a skirmisher you probably won't ever get close enough to an Indian to see them anyway."

"And if you're on horseback close enough to hit them," Smith said, "you won't have time to reload anyhow. Just whack them with the barrel and knock them around a bit."

"Why not use the saber if you're that close?" Donovan asked.

He got back one of those looks—three of them, actually—of tolerant amusement so often given to the uninitiated in any activity.

"We were given sabers because the regulations say we're supposed to have sabers. Don't expect to ever carry one into the field, though."

"Sabers are for dress parade. Period."

"Damn things are heavy, and they make a lot of noise rattling around. Nobody ever carries them on patrol."

"Just scrub the rust off yours," Sims said, "then put some grease on it and stick it someplace out of the way. You won't be needing it again unless the general comes to make an inspection."

"The general," Donovan repeated. "You mean *that* general?"

"One and the same," Smith said. "Not that any of us has ever seen him. And he's not really a general. He had a brevet during the war, so he was entitled to be called general then, but he's really a lieutenant colonel now. And he's not the CO of the regiment, either. Just the adjutant."

"But the commanding general, the real one I mean, is off in Washington doing something more important than bothering with the likes of us, so the general—they say he wants to be called that—is in charge more or less permanently."

"But not officially."

"I think I'm confused," Donovan said.

"That's all right. So is everybody else."

Donovan looked at the Spencer again. The carbine was short and amazingly heavy for so small a weapon. It was said to be reliable, though. And it was a repeater, one of the very few approved by the War Department.

The Spencer fired a .56-caliber rimfire self-contained cartridge and held seven of them in a tube that loaded at the back of the buttstock. A spring follower pushed the cartridges forward in the tube, and the trigger guard doubled as a lever to eject the spent brass and load a fresh round into the chamber.

To operate the gun—he had been taught by the other members of his four, as there was no formal instruction given on the subject—one pulled the trigger guard down and raised it again, then cocked the big hammer and took aim. The trigger pull was heavy and imprecise, and the sights were crude but adjustable—if one knew in which direction to adjust them.

"I sure would like to fire this a few times before I need it."

"Any ammunition for target practice would have to be paid for out of the captain's pocket," Sims said.

"And the captain ain't likely to do that," Gordon said.

"That'd be money better spent on something important."

"Whiskey, for instance."

"And don't try shooting that gun without permission, either. That would mean a court-martial and punishment. Buck and gag, ball and chain, maybe something a lot worse."

Donovan hefted the empty Spencer, held it to his shoulder, and took aim in the general direction of the horses on the picket line. "Oh, well. Maybe we won't ever see any Indians anyhow. That's what they said when I enlisted. They said the plains tribes are peaceable nowadays."

The other men of the four began to laugh. Too damn loudly, Donovan thought.

But then, maybe they knew something that he did not.

Chapter Five

It was mighty hard work being a trooper in the Seventh United States Cavalry, Donovan decided as he leaned backward in an attempt to stretch some of the kinks out of his badly aching back. His eyes burned from the salty sweat that was dripping into them, and his palms stung ferociously from the blisters he'd raised and broken there.

"What is this, Donovan? Time for your afternoon nap?"

Donovan did not bother looking in the corporal's direction. He wouldn't have liked what he saw there anyway. Instead, he once again picked up his ax and eyed the limbs yet to be removed from the newly felled tree. He and a man named Adams from Two Squad were limbing the trees that another fatigue crew dropped. Still others dragged the logs away and loaded them onto wagons for the haul back to Horan.

Someone in his wisdom had decided to make Camp

Horan a permanent installation on the Smoky Hill Road. And quite naturally they'd decided to move it several miles so all the effort of building dugouts and erecting tents could be abandoned and construction work started all over at this new location.

Donovan scowled and wiped a sweat-stinging hand over the leg of his bleached canvas fatigue trousers. To be perfectly fair about it, the decision was probably a sensible one. They'd moved the post closer to timber and reliable water. Now it sat on the east bank of a creek, just a little more than a rifle shot away from the woods that lined both sides of the water.

Trooper John Smith insisted the creek was called Smiths Creek. Donovan wasn't sure if Smith made the claim with a wink or if that really was the name. He didn't want to seem too gullible, so he refrained from asking.

"Donovan!" The corporal sounded peeved. But then, the corporal 'most always sounded peeved. Donovan whacked another small limb at its juncture with the trunk, then hit it again to chop it free. The logs would be cut into crude lumber to use in building barracks, stables, and officers' quarters, while the smaller limbs and slabs of removed bark would add to the supply of wood for heating and cooking. They said Kansas could be cold in the winter. Donovan rather wished they would get a sample of that now, when a bit of chill would be welcome. Kansas was damn sure hot enough in the summer; he could attest to that.

Adams chopped the last clump of small branches off the log they'd been trimming and whistled for the drag team to come take it away. There were no draft horses assigned to the troop, so they were having to use their cav mounts in harness. Donovan didn't much like that idea.

But looking on the bright side of things, maybe his assigned horse would founder or break a leg or something. Silver linings in dark clouds and all that sort of thing.

"This one next, d'you think?" Adams asked, pointing his ax at another of the many trees already downed and waiting to be trimmed.

"Whatever," Donovan told him. He grinned. "Or we could sit down and discuss the available choices first."

"Fine by me, but first you'd best go ask that loudmouth corporal what he thinks of the plan."

"This one," Donovan said, and began attacking the next tree with his ax.

Chapter Six

"God, my arms hurt," Donovan said as they stumbled back to the crudely assembled brush arbor that was serving as temporary quarters for the men. The officers' needs came first, of course. Then the horses'. The men—meaning enlisted men, as if officers were some exalted beings above and beyond the lowly designation of 'man'— would be attended to when nothing else needed to be done.

"All that swinging an ax," Sims sympathized.

"No, it's my hands that hurt from the ax. Sting like hell, they do. Blisters," Donovan said patiently. "It's that damned saber drill that's killing my arms. What'd we do today? Two hours? Three? I thought they'd never let be. And come to think of it, why are we spending all this time on saber drill, anyhow? I thought you told me we'd never have to use the things."

Sims grinned—but then he could; he'd been sent off on some other foolishness lately while the rest of the squad was busy cutting timber—and said, "We won't carry the sabers. Not to fight with, we won't. Trust me."

"But then why . . . ?"

Sims's grin got all the bigger. "It's simple, Trooper. The corporal knows that the sergeant is sure that the captain will worry that the major might want to show off for the colonel. Someday. Maybe. If the colonel ever decides to come this far away from the comforts back at Riley. Or wherever he is these days. You know. Just in case."

"So we learn the drill," Gordon put in from a few paces behind.

"Every day?" Donovan complained.

"If that's what we're told, sure. And why not? Do you have anything better to do with your time, Donovan?"

"Sleep comes to mind." That got a laugh from the other two.

"You can sleep come winter," Sims said. "That's what they told me last winter."

"You were with the Seventh last winter?" Donovan asked.

"Nah. The Seventh hadn't been formed then. But that's when I enlisted this time around." The wiry trooper grinned again. "Back into the damned infantry again. I should've known better. Let me tell you, son." Sims didn't look a month older than Donovan. But he'd been in the army longer. And he'd been in the war, wounded and everything. That seemed to give him the right to lecture Donovan. "You think the cavalry is bad, you ought to try the infantry. At least here they give us horses to ride. The infantry has to do all this same stuff and walk to and from the work details, too. Everybody says you shouldn't volunteer for anything ever. But when I heard they were taking guys for a new cav outfit, I piped up loud and clear mighty quick."

"Dang infantry has heavy rifles too. If you think the Spencer is heavy, just carry a Springfield around for a day," Gordon said.

"You came over from the infantry too?"

"Not me," Gordon told him. "I'm not that stupid." He looked at Sims and laughed. "I enlisted straight into the horse cavalry a couple months back when they put posters out looking for men who could ride and wanted some adventure."

Donovan smiled. "Yeah, I can see how a man would look at this as an adventure, all right. So what do you know about infantry rifles, then?"

"Jeez, Donovan, where have you been the past few years. Where I used to live, you could've gone around picking up discarded Springfield rifles by the wagon load and built picket fences just by jamming them in the ground by their bayonets."

Donovan was tempted to ask Gordon where that had been. But he remembered what Sims had told him before and bit the question back. It was entirely possible that Gordon had served before. In one army or perhaps the other. It wasn't something Donovan ever heard Gordon talk about. Sims was fairly open about his past service, which meant that he'd probably worn blue. Trooper John Smith volunteered nothing. And of course, no one asked. What with the name he carried now, Donovan more or less assumed that John Smith had once been a Confederate. If he had been, that would make him the first Johnny Reb—or used-to-be Reb—Donovan ever knew personally. Well, the first that he was aware of, anyhow. And of course it could be that Louie Gordon used to be one too. Donovan couldn't tell.

"How long do we have till evening stables?" Donovan asked as they reached the low, rickety shelter that was as close as they came to having a home right then.

"Not long enough for a snooze, if that's what you're thinking," Sims said.

Donovan sighed. "My arms sure hurt," he complained again as he dropped to his hands and knees so he could crawl inside the arbor to his blankets. Five minutes. Three. He just wanted to be able to lie down and close his eyes—if only for two minutes. Or one.

Chapter Seven

Patrol. His first. Despite his resolution to think, feel, and do nothing except what he was told, Donovan could not help but feel a distinct thrill of excitement at the prospect.

There was a certain . . . romance about it. Cavalry patrol. Riding out into hostile Indian country. A band of armed men, taking themselves into danger, duty bound to protect innocent travelers. Mounted patrol. There was something—an aura, a feeling, a hushed anticipation—that came with the orders. He found it, quite simply, impossible to avoid.

"What do you say, Donovan?" Sims called out from the other side of his horse. "Are you excited? Eager? Just a little bit scared, maybe?"

He was all of those things and more, but all he said was, "Dry up, will you," as he checked to make sure his cinches were tight and that the straps of the headstall weren't twisted. Error—one was all it had taken—proved that the horse, whose unofficial name was Handsome because he so patently wasn't, would react badly to an uncomfortable headstall, particularly if that discomfort were located anywhere on the left side of the homely animal's head, anywhere in the vicinity of the disfiguring scar left there by some musket ball or bayonet slash.

"Got your biscuits?" Sims asked.

Donovan glanced around to make sure the corporal wasn't near, then nodded.

The others had already warned him that when the Seventh took the field their rations were questionable as to quality and quantity alike, and a sensible trooper brought something extra. Allowable weight and accoutrements being severely limited, the troopers managed to carry something extra by making use of some of the space allotted to grain for their mounts. Each man was expected to carry a quantity of issue grain in his issue feed bag, tied at the left side of his issue saddle. The corporal could be expected to check and make sure that regulation was correctly followed on the subject.

What the corporal would *not* likely do was dump out the grain to inspect whatever might be found at the bottom of the feedbag. Most of the men carried leftover biscuits or hardtack crackers there to supplement their own diet. After all, the horses could fill up on the grass they walked over. And if it came to that, well, they could feed biscuits to the horses too. It was grain they were carrying in either case.

Donovan made sure his gear was in order, everything present, everything precisely where the corporal said it should be.

He made a final inspection of the Spencer carbine. It was loaded. For the first time actually, truly, genuinely loaded. There was no round in the chamber, of course. But the buttstock magazine was fully charged. Donovan felt . . . different . . . knowing the squad was armed and deadly now. He felt taller, stronger, more prepared to handle whatever came their way.

Scared spitless too, of course. But that was something else, wasn't it.

He looked down the picket line at the other members of his four and of his squad.

They all looked to be taking this as routine. Their faces betrayed no excitement. Certainly none of them looked fearful.

A sudden acute emptiness low in his belly reminded Donovan that he was the newcomer, the tenderfoot, the uninitiated.

These other men appeared calm, capable, and fearless.

God, he hoped if there was a scrap he would not let them down.

Better to take the savage's blows than to turn tail and let his messmates down.

God!

His plea was not a curse. It was a prayer.

"One Squad. Four Squad," the troop sergeant's voice bawled. "Form in twos. On me."

Donovan felt a rueful flutter in his gut as he reached down to untie Handsome from the troop's permanent picket line and lead him into their place at the back of Four Squad.

They were going in search of hostiles. Really going.

Jesus!

Chapter Eight

The night air felt chilly despite the flannel of his shirt and the wool of his jacket. Donovan shivered. From the cold, not from fear. He was not afraid. Not hardly. Bored, yes. But afraid? There was nothing to be afraid of. As far as he could tell, there was nothing within a hundred miles of them but grass and wildflowers, rabbits and redtail hawks. For the past two days that was all they'd seen: grass and more grass; wildflowers and more wildflowers; hawks soaring overhead in a cloudless sky and rabbits bolting underfoot.

Donovan suspected that the hawks deliberately followed the moving patrol, waiting above for the horses to flush game for the hawks to swoop—no, that wasn't the word he wanted. He had to think far back to something from a book read a long time ago. Stoop—that was it. A plummeting hawk or eagle was said to stoop onto its prey. He felt reasonably proud of himself for having remembered that.

But then, self-congratulation was only one of the many

wonderful amusements available to a man while he walked his tour of night guard.

Boring? To tears.

Stand for a while and shiver. Walk for a while. Stand some more. Oh, it was a gay and exciting life, this service in the horse cavalry.

Nearby he could hear the faint sounds of grass being torn by hard teeth as the horses idly cropped the lush prairie grasses and nipped at certain of the flowers.

Farther away there was the low drone of men snoring, those fortunates who were not walking guard at the moment.

There was no breeze to speak of—thank goodness, else the chill would have been magnified—but what little movement of air there was came from behind him, from the camp. He could smell the smoke from the evening's cook fires and a faint hint of pipe tobacco. Probably the sergeant of the guard, in this case One Squad's corporal, was awake and having a pipe to comfort him in the stillness of the night.

Donovan dutifully peered out across the rolling prairie. There was no moon, but starlight enough to make out shadow or movement—had there been anything out there to move or to throw a shadow.

Certainly they did not have to worry about hostiles. He'd begun to doubt they existed, not in this vast and empty sweep of country. Some of the boys said they would be down along the Arkansas. Others argued that by now the tribes would have abandoned their winter camps and be moving north to find buffalo for slaughter, and that the tribes should be up along the Platte.

Donovan had no idea which faction was correct. Or if both were wrong and the Indians were somewhere else entirely.

All he knew was that they were not present in this Smoky Hill country.

And that was just fine by him, thank you. Very fine indeed.

With a grunt and a sigh he transferred the stubby, dang-all heavy Spencer carbine from his left hand to his right and stuffed his aching left hand deep into his trouser pocket to keep warm.

He'd stood still long enough. It was time to walk some more.

Yes indeed, it was a thrilling life they led in the horse cavalry.

Chapter Nine

"Women!" Sims exclaimed. The topic was certainly common enough. The tone of voice was not. Donovan turned his head toward Sims, who was riding beside him, and licked dry lips before he answered. "You keep up thinking about the ladies, Ed, and you won't be getting any sleep tonight."

Sims pointed forward along the column and grinned. "Be hard not to think about them when there'll be some sleeping close enough we'll be able to smell them."

Donovan stood in his stirrups. Ahead two miles or a little more he could see some patches of white visible past the crest of a small rise. "Are those . . . ?"

"Ayuh. Prairie schooners, those be," Trooper Smith said eagerly. "Train of emigrants, sure enough."

"They 'most always have women with them," Gordon told him. "Lookers, some of them. Not the wives, o'course. Women always turn ugly, it seems, quick as they're married. But a lot of times there'll be girls traveling with their families, see. Pretty nice ones sometimes."

"Man, I been out here s' long," Sims moaned, "I wouldn't mind a fat, ugly old married woman."

"I don't want to hear none of that when we get over to those wagons," the corporal snarled. "You'll speak respectful around any womenfolk or face the captain when we get back."

Dang man has ears like a hawk has eyes, Donovan marveled silently. He had to admit, though, that the corporal wasn't on their backs so hard while they were out on patrol. On the parade ground a man had to sit like he had a ramrod up his backside and keep his mouth buttoned all the time. Away from post the corporal loosened up so much a man could come to think he was near to being human. That would be a mistake, of course. But the temptation was there.

As for the prospect of seeing a woman after all this time, well, that wasn't half bad.

"This your first time to see the movers, Donovan?" Sims asked.

"I saw a couple trains back around Independence, but that's about it. I've never spoken to any of them or anything like that."

"They aren't so bad, most of them. And they generally are real pleased to see us. They know they're safe while we're around, and that puts them into a good mood. Friendly. You know? One thing you got to keep in mind, though. From here they still have an awful way to go. Most of them don't really know what they're getting into. They're like to offer us coffee or beans or something. They'll be sincere as they can be, but don't you take none of them up on it. They go to giving their stuff away to soldiers, they're like to run out of supplies before they ever get across to California or Oregon or wherever. The rule is, you thank them real polite but don't you go taking any of what little they got. The army feeds us what we need." Sims shrugged and grinned. "Mostly."

"And if one of those unmarried girls offers me a kiss?" Donovan teased.

"That subject ain't never come up," Sims said.

"But if one does," Smith put in, "you come see me about what to do. I'll show you how to handle that."

The men laughed.

They also, all of them from the front of the short column all the way back, sat taller in their saddles, and almost imperceptibly the pace picked up as the men riding point began to let their horses stretch the gait just a little.

A body would almost think the men would be pleased to get over to where those wagons were stopped.

Chapter Ten

Oh, God. Oh, Jesus God in Heaven, Donovan moaned silently to himself. He could smell them. Oh, Jesus, he could smell them. Who'd said that? Sims, he thought. But . . . not like this. It wasn't supposed to be like this.

He could smell them. He could see them. He would see and smell them for the whole rest of his life. No one would ever be able to forget anything so awful as this was.

It was a train of emigrants, all right. It was wagon covers they'd seen from a distance.

But there was no one welcoming the patrol. There were no glad shouts of greeting, nor offers of coffee or dried fruit.

There was the stink of death and the sight of . . . of things worse than John Donovan would have been capable of imagining. And seeing it was worse than imagining ever could have been.

It was . . . horrid beyond contemplation.

He gazed at men, women, half-grown children, and

over there by that wagon even a baby. He'd mistaken the baby's body for a castaway rag doll. But it wasn't a doll stuffed with cloth. It was a child. A real one. Tiny and pale and lifeless, its little head shattered against the iron tire of a wagon wheel.

There were—he counted—eight wagons. Dozens of people. He didn't want to count those. Didn't want to have to look that closely. Dozens of them, though, he was sure about that.

And all of them dead.

Not just dead but horribly, brutally, savagely dead.

They'd been killed, their clothes stripped off them, the women raped, all of them scalped, all of them mutilated beyond Donovan's comprehension.

A rising breeze carried the stench of rot and expelled feces to him, and Donovan felt an impulse to puke. He tried to hold it back, then gave in and threw up.

He was not the only man in the column to do so.

The older men, though, the ones who'd seen such as this before, were not so affected.

"Listen up, people," the corporal said after a few moments of silence. "Look close here. This is why we're out here. This very thing." He paused and added, "If it makes you feel any better, look close again and pay attention to one thing. Bad as this looks—and it's bad, there's no mistake about that—bad as it looks, most of what was done to these people was done after they were already dead. If you look at them, you'll see that only some of those cuts and slashes show where blood has run. When a person's dead, the blood quits flowing. You see those slashes in that man's legs? They're bone deep and they're terrible to look at, but the meat on his thighs is cut as clean as slicing a roast of beef. Can you see that? The meat is laid open, but there's no blood has run out onto the skin. That man was dead and gone before some savage ever chopped him up like that. He never felt a thing."

"Will we be going after them, Corporal?" Thompson asked. Thompson was in another four but part of Donovan's squad.

"That's up to the sergeant. He's in charge."

It was well past the middle of the afternoon, and if they were going to pursue the Indians who'd slaughtered these people they surely would have to start after them soon, Donovan thought.

Instead the sergeant rode slowly through the wreckage of wagons and bodies. Nearly all human bodies, Donovan noted; there were only three dead horses on the ground, and two of those had been partially butchered for their meat. The rest of the horses had been stolen.

When the sergeant, who was leading the patrol out of Horan because there were not enough officers to go around, returned from an initial inspection of the scene he ordered the horses hobbled and pickets set out on perimeter guard. For the first time since Donovan joined N Troop, he hoped—desperately hoped—to be posted to guard detail. Anything in order to get farther away from this horror.

"You, You. Give your horses to your handlers. But take your cartridge boxes, mind. Stand picket on the west and south. The boys in One Squad can take the north and east."

Donovan was not one of the lucky pair the corporal pointed at.

"You and you. Go through the wagons. See if you can find shovels. Pickaxes. Whatever you can use to dig with."

Donovan felt his gorge rise again. They were not going to pursue. They would stay and bury the dead.

He could understand it, but he hated it nonetheless.

He walked shakily toward a wagon and had to pass close, too close, to the body of what had been a young woman. Perhaps a young and newly married woman who'd headed out on the great adventure of emigration in order to start a new life with a new husband. She'd found a hideous death instead.

She was naked now, exposed to eyes and insects and the burning glare of bright sunlight.

Donovan had never seen a naked woman before. He'd imagined one often enough but never actually seen one, and now he felt a sick sense of guilt when he looked at this dead woman's nakedness.

Her left breast was pale. A deep slash started on her chest and almost divided the flesh into two equal parts. Her right breast was missing entirely.

Her pubic hair, darker than the soft chestnut curls on her head, was clumped thick with matted blood.

Her stomach was sliced open and her face so battered that he had no idea what she might have looked like in life.

Yet he looked at her and felt a stirring of lust that under the circumstances disgusted him, and again he bent low to the ground and heaved, the taste of vomit sour in his mouth.

When he regained some small measure of control, he forced his eyes away from the young woman's body and hurried to the back of one of the wagons. The contents had been ransacked and everything that the marauders valued taken, but he found a soiled quilt that he carried back and spread over the woman's body, in an effort, however futile, to give her her dignity back.

Only then was he able to get on with the duties that were assigned to him. He cried silently while he did so, and if any of the other men noticed, they said nothing to him about it.

Chapter Eleven

Donovan's hands hurt where blisters formed and broke while they were preparing the long, deep mass grave that held the emigrants. No one knew their names to post. Not that there was any durable material available to chisel or carve names onto even if they had known. The patrol sergeant jabbed a singletree into the ground and propped a wagon tailgate against it.

"27 unknown movers buryed here 26 May 18 and 67 killed by indians May God have mercy on their souls" was written onto the boards with ink that had been found in one of the wagons. The ink would quickly weather away, and soon enough Donovan supposed all trace of the grave would disappear. But, however poor, it was the best they could do.

Worse, though, they'd been unable to find much in the way of stones to pile on top of the mounded dirt that marked the site. He doubted they would be much more than over the horizon before wild things began to dig and to burrow in order to get at the dead. Coyotes, foxes, mice, and rats . . . there was no telling what might be able to reach them. And once the fur-bearers exposed the bodies, the birds would come. It was a disquieting thought.

"Mount up." The sergeant sounded weary. Back at Horan his voice had been strong and forceful when it rang out on the parade ground. Here he sounded as sad as Donovan felt, and his voice was small in the great emptiness that surrounded them.

Donovan felt a stirring of passion as he swung onto the saddle, very much aware of the weight of his carbine in its shoulder sling. He settled his boots comfortably into the stirrups and made sure the barrel of the Spencer rested deep into the leather socket attached to his saddle, giving the weight of the weapon to the ring of leather instead of his shoulder.

He touched the breech of the Spencer to reassure himself that it was ready to hand. For a moment he wished they'd brought the heavy, cumbersome sabers this time. The thought of slashing a murdering savage's face and neck was enticing.

But then they probably would not be able to get close to the war party even if they did catch up with them. The other boys all said the Indian ponies were quick. But they could be worn down—the grass-fed horses hadn't the endurance of the much heavier cav mounts, or so Sims and the others claimed. If, that is, the grain held out.

The patrol had been out four days now, and their meager supply of grain was exhausted.

But surely, Donovan thought, the American horses had strength and stamina enough for a few hard days' march.

In any event, they would have to make the attempt.

Donovan tried to prepare himself for the possibility of actual fighting. The idea was not as hard to accept now as it might have been.

He sat with grim determination as he saw the sergeant lean nearer the men who'd been chosen to ride point for the day. He saw the sergeant's lips move as the man gave orders, turned his head to spit a stream of dark tobacco juice, and then turned back to snap a harsh response to something one of the outriders said.

Moments later Donovan understood why the outriders, both of them, looked so unhappy with the orders they'd received.

The marauders had ridden north, out onto the buffalo plains, after they had slaughtered the innocent travelers.

The trail that would lead to their discovery and punishment led in that direction.

But the point riders moved out to the south and east. Back toward Camp Horan.

"Jesus!" Donovan blurted.

John Smith's curse was vulgar but carried the same sentiment.

"We aren't gonna chase them," Louie Gordon moaned. "We aren't even gonna try."

"I don't believe it," Sims grumbled.

"Shut up," the corporal barked. "All of you shut the hell up back there." But Donovan couldn't help notice that the corporal sounded as unhappy as the rest of them were.

The patrol sergeant waited until the point riders were half a mile out, then waved for the column to follow. "For'ard ho."

With a muted thud of hoofbeats and jangle of equipment, the patrol left the grave and the ransacked wagons standing forlorn and bleak on a featureless prairie.

Donovan wished they could leave the memory behind as easily.

Chapter Twelve

Donovan watched the messenger ride on, not back toward the post, but farther up creek to where a wood-cutting detail was felling timber. He wasn't so much interested in the messenger, a man from Three Squad who'd earned the light duty by coming tops at inspection last Sunday, as he was in having an excuse to stand upright and straighten his back.

He'd been assigned to the sawyer's pit for the morning and was standing precariously atop a rickety scaffold, straddling a mostly straight section of log and dragging the top end of an eight-foot-long steel saw while in the pit below a trooper named Mills handled the downhaul. The two-inch-thick slabs of raw wood would be allowed briefly to dry and then be used—or so rumor said—to construct a mess hall for the troop.

A real mess hall with tables and condiments and food prepared in an actual kitchen would be an achievement, and Donovan did not mind the task. But that didn't stop his back from aching.

"All right, everybody. Stop what you're doing. Form up."

"What's up, Nesbitt?" someone called out to the One Squad corporal who was in charge of the lumber detail.

"We're recalled to post," Nesbitt shouted back. "Now form up, will you? Everybody up."

Trouble was Donovan's first thought. But he was mistaken. As the dozen men in the detail slowly assembled, Corporal Nesbitt was grinning. "Pay call this afternoon. Everybody's to get cleaned up and out of the canvas. It's clean blues and inspection this afternoon. Pay after."

"No kidding," somebody said eagerly.

"No kidding," the corporal affirmed.

Donovan had been at Horan almost three months now, and this would be his first pay call. They told him the army was meticulous with its accounting, but not particularly punctual as to delivery, and a monthly payday was something enjoyed only by those lucky few who were assigned to the older and larger established garrisons like Leavenworth or Riley or down south at Larned. Camp Horan wasn't more than a pimple on the plains and was seldom visited.

"Bertram says we're getting more people too. Another troop maybe. Said he could see them coming. At least one full troop, supply wagons, the paymaster, all kinds of newcomers on their way in."

Bertram. That would be the messenger, Butch. Everybody knew the youngster from Three Squad as Butch, but Corporal Nesbitt had found out that the serious young trooper's proper name was Bertram and insisted on calling him that. Nesbitt didn't like Butch for some reason.

What mattered now, though, had nothing to do with

petty disagreements within the troop. Payday. That was pretty exciting.

Nesbitt did not need to urge the men to hurry as they carried their tools and hardware back to the post. The work left undone today could be finished tomorrow. Now there were baths to take and very-best uniforms to pull out from beneath the mattresses that kept them as close to being pressed as it was possible to make them. There would be a mad scramble for the last scraps of shaving soap, and efforts made to tame hair left unkempt since the last inspection. Boots would be blacked and buttons scrubbed with sand and spit.

Payday.

Not that there was anything to spend it on out here.

But . . . payday.

Chapter Thirteen

"What is all *this*, I ask you?" For once the corporal didn't bark about talking in the ranks. This time it was the corporal himself who'd blurted aloud the same thing the whole squad was thinking.

Out along the track—the way hadn't been used anywhere near enough yet to form ruts that might someday be called a road—there were men in blue. And more men in blue. And damned if it didn't look like a passel of civilian wagons to boot.

"Infantry!" someone in the squad marveled.

"Quiet!" the corporal snapped. But he was undoubtedly noticing the same thing, and his heart wasn't in the reprimand.

It was true though. Leading the long, winding file of arrivals was what looked like half a troop of cavalry, but strung out behind them and lagging far enough back to stay out of the small amount of dust that was being raised by the horses was a double file of actual, honest-to-Pete

46

infantry, unwieldy rifles and all. Behind the infantry was an ambulance—undoubtedly the regimental paymaster—with a mounted guard front and rear. And behind that were a string of freight wagons, a round dozen of them. Trailing the whole shebang was a final squad of cavalry.

It took quite a while for them all to come into view, and by the time they were sure there was nothing more to be seen, the first of the advance unit was coming near to the post. A trooper mounted on an exceptionally tall horse led the way with a guidon proclaiming the unit was 7/B—B Troop of the 7th Cav Regiment.

The boys of N gave a rousing cheer when B Troop arrived, and not a noncom in the crowd said or did a thing to discourage them. But then, the noncoms would be drawing pay today too.

Officers on horseback milled around and shouted orders and waved and pointed and in general added to the confusion.

Eventually they worked it out for B Troop to start erecting a picket line for their mounts over near the half-built N Troop stables, and for the infantry to start setting up a bivouac on the opposite side of the camp from the cavalry.

The wagons were directed into a makeshift park, which Donovan heard a couple of the boys call a laager, established at the far end of the camp more or less opposite officers' country across the broad flat that they'd been using as a parade ground.

Until now the new Camp Horan had been roughly L-shaped, with N Troop strung out north to south and the officers' accommodations at the north end and running east to west. Now the infantry was spread along the east side of the newly formed quadrangle and the civilian wagons closed it all in at the south.

That was all interesting enough.

But the normal excitements of payday and the introduction of strangers was nothing compared to what came next.

The canvas cover of the next-to-last freight wagon was pulled open, and civilians emerged from within.

Six civilians.

Six *female* civilians.

"My God, boys," the top sergeant was overheard to reverently breathe, "we got us some laundresses."

The top soldier's gaffe was greeted with an outburst of cheering that would have made a full regiment proud, never mind one puny little troop.

Chapter Fourteen

"Damn infantry," somebody complained. "They've had all this time to cozy up to the women."

"That's all right," someone else responded. "What those women got don't wear out."

"Besides," Trooper John Smith added, "better for them to do the work of building the laundry than us, right?"

That was, they all conceded, one positive thing about having a company of infantry at the post. There were more hands to perform the labor that needed doing. And everyone knew that infantrymen were nothing but broad backs and empty heads. Better they should do the work than bold cavalrymen.

The line of cavalry troopers shuffled a pace forward in the hot, heavy air of late afternoon. The whole troop, probably without exception, was lined up to gain access to a wagon that had a signboard propped against its wheels proclaiming "E. A. Erickson, Post Sutler."

There were no infantrymen in the line. Only the boys

of N Troop. Donovan guessed the plain-leg walks-a-heap soldiers—the boys said that's what the Indians called the infantry—had received and already blown their pay before they ever arrived at Horan.

Well, now it was the cavalry's turn, and he was looking forward to it. Lordy, he surely was.

The line crept forward, and Donovan's thoughts wandered so far from Kansas that he was surprised when he found himself facing a florid old man of fifty or more with bushy gray sidewhiskers and a face streaked with sweat.

"What d'you need, Trooper?"

"Um. Thread. I need some thread. And a paper of needles. And . . ."

"Dammit, man, don't waste my time. You can buy notions, foods, things like that tomorrow. Now, do you want some liquor or don't you?"

"Oh, I . . . uh . . . a beer, please." Donovan smiled. "I'd like a beer."

The old man—Donovan assumed he must be Erickson—snorted and looked past Donovan's shoulder to Sims, who was in line behind him.

"What about . . . ?"

"Do you think I'm going to haul barrels of beer all the way out here? You want beer, you'll have to go back to the States to find it. All I carry is trade liquor for you people and bonded whiskey or brandy for the officers. Now, either buy something or get out of the way."

"I, um . . ."

"Yes or no? Hurry up, man."

Donovan thrust his cup forward and the civilian poured a scant dipper of colorless liquid into it.

"That'll be ten cents," Erickson snapped.

Donovan paid and stepped out of the way. He was disappointed. Still, it was payday. He should feel good about that.

He carried his cup of liquor—the man might call it whiskey, but it tasted awful; it carried the heat of raw alcohol but not the flavor of a decent whiskey—out away from camp, wandering in no particular direction but wanting of a sudden to find some privacy out on the great, empty expanse of grass that surrounded them.

Behind him he could hear the clang of metal on metal, the occasional shout or gleeful, whiskey-fueled yell, and underlying the other sounds the plaintive calls of sentry posts reporting their routine "All's well" signals as dusk turned into night.

Funny, he thought, how a man could be surrounded by so many others and yet feel so alone.

Chapter Fifteen

"The fat one. Did you get the fat one?"

"Naw, the line for her was too long. I went with the old broad with the big . . ." The trooper cupped both hands in front of his chest and mimed weighing something large and heavy there.

The other boys laughed, then leaned forward with great excitement to relate their own experiences.

The sole topic of discussion this morning was the laundresses who'd arrived yesterday. Them and their various carnal attributes.

To listen to the boys of N Troop, Donovan thought, you would think their adventures of the previous evening some sort of amorous conquest instead of simple commercial transactions. Their encounters were to romance the exact same thing as wielding a hammer in a packing house was to the sport of hunting. Not that anyone else seemed to notice the difference. Or care.

Donovan didn't actually care himself. But he was

mildly amused by the excitement with which these morning-after tales were told.

"Which one did you have, Donovan?" Sims asked with the poke of a sharp elbow into his ribs.

He only shrugged and smiled. Obviously no one had noticed that he hadn't participated in the payday revelry. A single cup of the so-called whiskey—it was so genuinely awful that the taste did not improve as the bottom of the cup was reached—and a long walk had been enough of a celebration to satisfy.

Now nearly the entire troop was badly hung over, their eyes red and legs wobbly. Morning mess call had been a complete waste. Practically no one was able to stomach the chunks of greasy bacon and hard biscuit served to those few who even made an attempt at eating.

Donovan would have thought the choice of food cruel except for one thing: Breakfast for N Troop was always greasy bacon and hardtack. Fortunately, he liked bacon. And this morning he had access to all he wanted, his own portion and that of half the rest of the squad too. Some of it he'd eaten and the rest he wrapped in a cloth and put away to enjoy later. Most of the boys, those who bothered to come to breakfast at all, could stomach only hardtack soaked in coffee. For a bacon lover, the day was starting out fine.

Out on the parade ground the troop bugler put in a belated appearance. The wonder was that Zim—Donovan couldn't recall his proper name, but it began with a Z—could walk upright this morning. He certainly hadn't been able to last night.

The first notes were a meaningless sputter of metallic noise that slowly evolved into something approximating the call to stables.

"Time to go to work, boys," Donovan said with a

bright and brittle note of good cheer that drew a round of groans from the others.

Payday, he thought. Quite a spectacle, all things considered.

Chapter Sixteen

"Donovan!"

"Yes, Corporal."

"Your horse's feet are filthy. Looks like you haven't cleaned them in a week."

"I cleaned them just this morning, Corporal."

"I don't want to hear any sass from you, dammit. Your smart-aleck back talk makes it the worse. Company punishment, Donovan. See me after retreat. You'll carry the log. Thirty minutes."

"Yes, Corporal."

When the corporal had gone grumbling and complaining away, Donovan looked at the man next to him on the woodcutting detail. "What was that all about?"

"Rathburn has a case of the red-ass," Hec Parker responded. "Way I hear it, the captain is royally pissed because they gave command of the post to that infantry major. The captain, he expected to get command. So now he's mad. He spent half of last night, until he passed out anyway, chewing on the first sergeant. This morning the top soldier passed it along to the squad corporals. And now it looks like Rathburn picked you to carry his share."

"Lucky me," Donovan said with a groan and a rolling of his eyes.

"Ever carry the log before?"

Donovan shook his head.

"Lemme give you a tip. When Rathburn takes you over to the woodpile to pick one, don't pick the smallest. If you do, he'll make you carry one twice as heavy. Pick the third or maybe even fourth smallest. He might let you get away with that."

"Thanks."

Parker only shrugged and, with a sideways cant of his eyes toward the corporal, went back to work sawing eight-foot trunk sections into stove-length chunks ready for splitting.

Later, when the rest of the squad was relaxing out back of the newly completed barracks, Donovan reported to the squad corporal as ordered.

Rathburn looked him over with a critical eye, his expression stating as plainly as words could have done that it would please him no end if he could find a button missing or Donovan's shirttail hanging out.

Sims had already warned him about that, thank goodness, and although in stable fatigues he'd dressed as carefully as if preparing for guard mount. Now he stood at rigid attention while the unhappy corporal inspected him.

"All right, dammit. Pick a log."

"Yes, Corporal." He'd already looked the lot over and without hesitation bent to the third-smallest chunk of unsplit wood he could see. He guessed it weighed twenty pounds or more.

"Not that one," Rathburn barked.

Donovan straightened and looked the man in the eye but said nothing.

"That one." The corporal pointed.

Donovan stifled an impulse to object. The chunk wasn't only big at probably something close to forty pounds, it was awkward too, the sides rough and irregular in shape with many stubs from which small branches had been cut. "Yes, Corporal." He picked the thing up. It was a bitch to carry, badly shaped and with the bulk of its weight at one end that was thicker than the other.

"Overhead, Donovan. Arms extended. And don't let me see those arms come down or your time will double. D'you understand me, Donovan?"

"Yes, Corporal." He gritted his teeth, finding it near about all he could do to keep his resentment hidden.

"All right, now. Around the parade ground. Double time, ay? Thirty minutes, and not ten seconds less. I'll be right here counting."

"Yes, Corporal." He'd been holding the log overhead for—what . . . twenty seconds or so?—and already he could feel the strain in his arms. Thirty minutes. He didn't think he could do it.

But he'd be damned if he would let Rathburn best him. Whatever the stinking corporal could dish out, Donovan could take and then some, damn the man.

With a deep breath and a tight jaw, he began a slow jog counterclockwise around the parade ground.

Chapter Seventeen

"Here." Sims held out a quart-sized, cork-stoppered bottle that held something that looked black and oily.

"What is that?"

"Liniment. I got it from Hanratty." Hanratty was the troop's farrier sergeant, charged not only with shoeing the horses but with any veterinary care that was beyond the ability of the troopers.

Donovan gave the bottle a skeptical look. "Horse medicine?"

"It works," Sims told him. "Stinks. But it works."

"I don't think so, thanks." The truth was that he didn't think he could move his arms enough to take the bottle, twist the cork out, and apply the liniment to his own burning arms and aching shoulders. He was limp. Used up. How he'd managed the final minutes holding that cursed log aloft he did not know. Afterward he'd come back to the newly built barracks and collapsed, not even bothering to join the others for the evening meal. He had the leftover bacon put by. He would eat that later if he felt up to it.

Sims looked at him closely and must have guessed the problem. "Can you get your shirt off by yourself?"

Donovan thought about it for a moment and then, responding honestly, shook his head.

Sims set the liniment aside and opened the buttons for him, peeled the shirt off Donovan's back, and then pulled the cork out of the bottle. He was right, Donovan thought, wrinkling his nose. The liniment stank. "What's that stuff made of?"

"Fermented buffalo piss." Sims grinned and shrugged. "I dunno. Doesn't matter what's in it so long as it works, does it?" He poured some of the thick, nasty liniment into his palm and began rubbing it into Donovan's shoulders and upper arms. Almost instantly he could feel a warmth seep into his muscles. Warmth. And then outright heat almost to the point of pain.

Still, the heat of the liniment was nothing compared with the misery he'd earned from the log. And in another thirty seconds or so that pain seemed quite genuinely diminished.

"Lordy, that feels good. Thanks."

"I been there. It won't last. Couple, three days and you won't hardly know it. Week or so and you'll not even be able to remember it."

"Thanks," Donovan said again.

"Tomorrow," Sims said, "you hang back. Everybody knows you carried the log this evening. Tomorrow you drive the wagon if we're sent out on detail."

"What about Rathburn? What if he tells me to swing an ax or something? I don't . . . I really don't think I could do it, Sims. I don't think I could." Refusal of an order . . . failure to perform his duty . . . he had no idea what depth of trouble that would bring.

"You won't have to. Rathburn won't make all the assignments tomorrow. That way he don't have to assign you to drive. Doing that, see, would be like doing you a favor, and he won't do that. Not after making you carry the log. But he won't make you do anything else, either. That's the way it works. He won't tell anybody to drive, and the other boys know enough to not say anything and nobody else will step up to do the driving. Comes the time, you just crawl up on that wagon and take the lines. The rest of us, we'll take care of the cutting and the loading."

"Thanks, I . . ."

"You'll do the same for the next man. That's all."

Donovan nodded.

Sims finished rubbing the smelly, uncomfortable, blessedly relieving liniment into Donovan's abused muscles, then jammed the cork back into the bottle and gruffly said, "I got to get this back to Hanratty. Here, now." Sims dropped a packet of something light and bulky, wrapped in greasy paper, onto Donovan's bunk and hurried away.

The paper proved to contain a full serving of corn bread brought over from the mess. Probably Sims's own ration of the rare and highly prized fresh-made corn bread.

Donovan felt infinitely better than before. The improvement, however, had little to do with the lessening of pain and much to do with the kindness that had brought about the small measure of physical relief.

Chapter Eighteen

Sims was right. It wasn't so bad now. This was his third day on the wagon, and he figured tomorrow he would grab a saw out of the toolshed and go do some proper work for a change. He didn't want anyone to think he was using company punishment as an excuse to get out of work. All the other boys had to work. So should he.

It wasn't so bad now anyway, the amount of stuff that had to be done. The infantry, poor clodbusting plain-leg souls, were there to cut timber for their own barracks just like the boys of N Troop'd had to do. And once all the post buildings were erected the infantry would be available to swap off the firewood detail too. That wouldn't be so bad. More hands always make for lighter work, Donovan believed.

Another improvement with the coming of the infantry was the presence of their baggage train. The bigger, heavier wagons arrived pulled by bigger, heavier horses, and that meant the troop's light cav mounts no longer had to serve in harness for the wood hauling.

That was good news. Word was the Indians were on the move in large numbers again as the grass and the weather improved, so Camp Horan and N Troop would be riding out on more patrols as the approaching summer brought both hostiles and emigrants into the Smoky Hill country. They would need the horses to be in good condition for that. He had no idea what use infantry would be when it came to protecting the emigrant trains. They'd probably just stay around the post, Donovan supposed, and do the housekeeping chores necessary so the real soldiers, the cavalry, could be out chasing hostiles and protecting innocent travelers.

Thinking about that brought a flash of memory into Donovan's thoughts like a daguerreotype, but in full color and awful detail, of that dead young woman he'd seen out on the road last month.

In his mind's eye he could still see her. And he was again both repulsed and aroused by the memory.

Forcing that memory out of his mind led him only to a worse thought. That was of the post laundresses. So far he'd avoided them. He'd listened to the other boys' tales, though. He couldn't have kept from hearing their ribald accounts if he'd wanted to. And the truth was that, well, he didn't really want to. He was fascinated by the things they said. When they talked, the thoughts their words conjured up inside him were exciting and at the same time more than a little dismaying.

He wished, actually, that their stories were more detailed and graphic than was the case. He really would have liked to ask questions. What did it mean when they said this? How did one go about doing—well—that?

How was a fellow supposed to act? Just exactly what was it that he was supposed to do? And what would the laundresses do in return? Big questions like those. And littler ones like what a reasonable price was and when the money was to be paid.

Donovan felt himself an ignoramus and, worse, knew of no way to arrive at this yearned-for knowledge without making himself the butt of barracks humor.

Dammit. He . . .

He sat taller on the wagon seat and looked about. He must have run over a nest of hornets or something, because he could hear a swarm of them buzzing overhead. In ones and twos they passed him, none coming all that close, but close enough to make him just a little bit nervous. He was feeling fit again after the misery of carrying the log for the corporal and didn't want a bunch of wasp stings to make him start hurting all over now.

The thought of being stung made his ears and the back of his neck feel all creepy-crawly, and he leaned forward and clucked to his team to get them to move along a little more quickly. The wagon was empty, on its way back to the woodlot, so there was no reason the animals couldn't step it out a little more quickly.

Donovan pursed his lips and let out a shrill whistle. The near horse swiveled its ears and tossed its head in mild annoyance, but it also lengthened its stride. Its heavier and less responsive companion matched the leader's gait as exactly as if the two were images in a mirror.

Off to Donovan's left, somewhere across the creek, he could hear a crackle and snap as of breaking wood, and out in front of him he could see some of the boys from the squad waving and jumping up and down.

For a moment Donovan wondered if they thought he

was bringing something out to them. A late-morning snack, perhaps. He hadn't gone and forgotten a favor or an errand somebody'd asked him to do, surely. Lordy, he hoped not.

He tried to think of anything anyone might have said—Rathburn in particular—but he couldn't call anything like that to mind. No, he was pretty sure he wasn't supposed to fetch anything back out from the post except himself and the empty wagon ready for the next load of cut wood.

He couldn't think of . . .

More of those damned hornets went by. And more snapping and popping came from across the creek.

And now in front of him some of the boys had grabbed up their carbines and were aiming them over in that direction.

He could see the cottonball puffs of smoke belching out of the muzzles of the Spencers and hear the snap and crackle of the gunshots, and. . . .

Jesus God! Snap and pop. Just like he'd been hearing from across the creek. That wasn't somebody breaking wood over there. It was gunfire. Actual, honest-to-Pete *gun*fire.

Indians. Hostiles. Had to be. Some of the sons of bitches had come by to take potshots at the wood detail.

And they were shooting at him.

Donovan ducked low and lashed the backs of his team with the driving lines, shouting for the horses to break into a run.

Jesus God!

Chapter Nineteen

He was shaken. Shaking, too. Literally. His knees felt like India rubber when he crawled unsteadily down off the wagon seat.

The other boys on the woodcutting detail were grinning now, and there wasn't any shooting going on, so he supposed the Indians had had their fun and left once the troopers started shooting back.

"First time you been shot at, Donovan?" Hec Parker asked.

He didn't trust his voice to answer without giving his fear away, so he settled for nodding his response.

"Fun, ain't it?" Ed Sims put in.

"Come close, did they?" one of the One Squad boys asked. Donovan didn't know the man's right name, but he thought they called him Bud.

Donovan looked off across the creek, out toward where the Indians had been. "Close enough. I . . . that's the awfullest sound in the world, those bullets coming by like that."

"No," Sims said softly, "the awfullest sound is one of them bullets hitting live meat."

Donovan shuddered.

"Aw, hell," Parker said, "Indians can't hit nothing. They make a lotta noise, but they never hit nothing."

Donovan thought about the horrors they'd seen at that wagon train massacre but didn't say anything aloud. They never spoke of that for some reason. He hadn't particularly noticed that fact before, but now he realized it was true. None of them who'd seen that awful sight ever spoke of it. None of them, not even the old vets from back in the war, and surely they'd seen as bad and maybe even worse. It was almost like those emigrants never existed.

Or like their deaths didn't matter.

"All right, dammit," the corporal bawled at the men who'd gathered close around Donovan and the wood wagon. "Get back at it, the lot of you. You've got no coffee that needs cooling, so shut your mouths and get to cutting."

Rathburn glared at Donovan but this time did not single him out.

It took two attempts to climb back onto the wagon before Donovan could gather up his lines again and get the team to turn and back into place.

A detail consisting mostly of men from Three Squad began pitching lengths of cut, but as yet unsplit, log sections into the bed.

Chapter Twenty

Vinegar. Donovan had never really appreciated vinegar before. In truth, he'd never particularly thought about vinegar before now. But he'd certainly learned to appreciate and think about it.

Now that there was a sutler to buy nonissue extras from, the mess was able to use the accumulated troop fund—they deducted sixty-five cents out of each man's monthly pay as his contribution to the troop fund, whether he liked it or not—and provide the boys with some niceties. Like condiments. Not that there was so very much available. But now they had vinegar to liven up the flavor of the beans or to hide the nitrate sting of half-spoiled salt pork.

They had regular vinegar. They had vinegar that was steeped in hot peppers. They even had pickles every Sunday dinner.

And they had sugar. Real sugar, lumpy and dark and

without the sulfur undertaste that molasses always left behind.

It was wonderful. Donovan had almost forgotten that food could have flavor to it.

"Pass that vinegar, will you?"

Louie Gordon reached for the bottle, liberally anointed his own plate of red beans swimming in too much juice, then passed the vinegar along to Donovan.

Oh, this was fine, Donovan thought as the sharp, biting odor of the vinegar reached him. He splashed the wonderful stuff onto his beans and handed the bottle on.

Life out here wasn't all bad, he acknowledged as he packed a heaping spoonful of beans into his mouth.

Chapter Twenty-one

Donovan was sore. It wasn't the riding that was causing it. Not exactly. The saddle and the riding really didn't bother him. His problem was a pimple. At least he hoped it was a pimple. It certainly felt like one. The reason he was not positive about that, though, was that the sore—pimple—was in a place that he could reach but not see. And two days in the saddle, riding out on patrol, was making it worse. If he'd had some more of that liniment or some other of the farrier sergeant's magical concoctions he would have tried them, but Three and Four Squads were out on their own. One and Two and all the support personnel were lying about back at Camp Horan.

Not that Donovan or any of the rest of them considered themselves to be lying about when they were the ones left at Horan. They had to do all the hard physical labor that was required in garrison while the others were out lollygagging around in the field, enjoying the movement and

69

the freedom of roving patrol duty. Funny how it always worked out that way.

Now Donovan rather wished he'd invented some sickness that would have kept him in garrison when the rest of the squad rode out. His butt was just so sore that . . .

"Dammit!" The voice came from the back of the loose column of twos.

Up at the front Rathburn looked back, scowled, and called out, "Column"—at which point everyone sat up a little straighter and took a tighter hold on their reins—"halt." The column of twenty men—the others were riding point and flank—came to a stop at very nearly the same time. Pretty darn good for not being on the parade ground, Donovan thought.

Rathburn, who'd been put in charge of the patrol on account of the first sergeant and officers all having the vapors or some such, rode to the back of the column while the rest of the men quite naturally turned in their saddles to see what the problem was.

The problem was Butch Anderson, the earnest young trooper from Three Squad. Or, more accurately, it was Butch's horse. The animal had come up lame. It stood with one hoof lifted completely off the ground. Butch was standing beside it with a worried look about him. He said something that Donovan couldn't hear.

He could hear Rathburn's reply easily enough. The corporal had a voice that grated on a man's ear and carried even when he wasn't trying to speak out. Donovan believed, but hadn't yet tested his theory, that Rathburn's whispers could be overheard from clean across the Camp Horan parade ground. He intended to verify that if Rathburn ever tried to whisper. So far that hadn't ever happened.

"What the hell were you doing so far out from the column that your horse could step in a damned hole like that? Can you explain that to me, Trooper? How come everybody else passed right on by but your mount stepped in the hole? Eh, Trooper?"

Butch said something and looked apologetic, but there wasn't much else he really could say about it. It had happened, that's all, and the patrol leader's bitching wasn't going to change it.

Growling and grumbling under his breath — so maybe, Donovan conceded, the man's whispers *couldn't* be overheard from indefinite distances—Rathburn dismounted. He glared at the rest of the men, every one of whom was staring at him, and in a peeved tone announced, "Dismount. Loosen your cinches and let the horses blow." Then he turned back to Butch and his horse.

Rathburn picked up the injured foot. The horse tried to shy away, but Rathburn held on to the leg and used his free hand to feel it.

"Busted," he announced. He gave Butch a murderous look. "Do you know how much it costs the Army to replace a trained cavalry horse?"

"I dunno," Butch said with a grin. "What's it cost to ship one of the poor old wore-out things out here from the tannery?"

"I don't want any of your damned lip, Trooper." Rathburn turned his attention to Three Squad's corporal, a cocky little SOB—being a son of a bitch seemed a prerequisite for earning a noncom's stripes, or so Donovan was told—named Irving. Rathburn motioned for Irving to join him. "It's broken, all right, Irv. Your squad and your man. I expect you should give the order."

"Shoot the horse, Anderson," Irving ordered.

71

"Corporal, I . . . I can't do that."

"You damn well can, mister. You busted his leg. Now you put him down."

Butch looked about as thoroughly miserable as Donovan had ever seen a person get. He very reluctantly lifted his Spencer, which was dangling at his side on the sling.

"No, dammit, take the saddle and gear off first," Irving corrected. "We aren't going to abandon that out here."

It occurred to Donovan to wonder what they were going to do with an extra saddle and other tack—and, for that matter, what they would do about having one man on foot. They didn't take any spare mounts along on patrol, and no wagon ever could have kept up. Nor could a man on foot.

Butch unhappily removed all his gear from the horse and, tears plainly visible in his eyes, levered a cartridge into the chamber of his Spencer. He cocked the carbine and placed the muzzle behind the ear of the patiently standing brown horse. From where he stood beside old Handsome, Donovan could see that Butch shut his eyes tight a split second before he squeezed the trigger.

The report of the .56-caliber cartridge seemed unnaturally loud in the silence of the empty plains. The horse didn't so much as jerk or throw its head. It simply dropped straight down to the ground like a marionette whose strings somebody had let go of.

Butch gave the dead animal a stricken look, then ran his sleeve under his nose and let the Spencer fall to the end of his sling. He didn't say anything. Didn't look at either of the corporals.

"Pick up your gear, Trooper," Rathburn ordered.

"What about . . . ?" Irving inclined his head in Butch's direction.

"We have our orders. We aren't going to change them just because of one man. We'll resume the patrol. Anderson, you'll walk back to post. And when you get there you damn well better have every piece of equipment that was issued to you. D'you understand that? Corporal Irving will be inspecting your gear when we get back, and it'd better all be there. Do you understand me, Trooper?"

"Yes, Corporal."

"All right, then." In a louder voice Rathburn called out, "Patrol. Prepare to mount."

The men, Donovan included, quickly yanked on their reins to pull their horses away from the tufts of prairie grasses they'd been munching, and then hurried into position beside the left stirrup of their own saddles.

"Mount!" Rathburn ordered, and as one—well, almost so—the men of Four and Three Squads swung into their saddles.

"At the walk. Forward . . . ho."

They set off again, leaving Anderson alone probably . . . Donovan tried to guess as best he could . . . fifty or sixty miles west by north from Camp Horan. A man might as well be in the darn infantry if he was going to have to walk that far.

Chapter Twenty-two

"I tell you, boys, I didn't like it out there by myself. Not even a little bit, I didn't." Butch was holding forth from the foot of his bunk—real bunks they were, too, iron-frame ones that had come in on the last bunch of government wagons sent out from Fort Riley—filling in all the troopers who'd been out on the patrol with him.

Butch had been there waiting for them when the patrol got back. "Tell you the truth, it was scary. Wolves or some such yapping half the night. Shadows moving every which way. Never knowing when some Injun might pop up and decide to take my hair.

"I reckon I woulda give a good account of myself first, 'least until I run out of ca'tridges. But what could one man do against a bunch of savages, huh? I tell you true, I was scared and I don't mind saying it. Wasn't right of your damned corporal to set me out afoot like that." He gave the boys from Four Squad an accusing look, as if they were responsible for what Rathburn did.

"I walked for three days. Can you believe it? Three days like that. You got any idea how much a damn Spencer carbine weighs? And my saddle and stuff, too?" He shook his head. "Damn things got heavier by the hour, let me tell you."

"You were lucky," one of the Three Squad troopers said. "Lucky you didn't see any Indians."

"I think maybe I did. Saw some riders afar off. That was on the first day, and I wasn't to the road yet. I was just headed for it, and passing at an angle off in front of me and heading pretty much the same way was this bunch of riders. Well, I knew you boys had gone the other way altogether, so it wasn't the patrol. And there wasn't wagons or anything with them. I figure they was prob'ly Injuns."

"What'd you do, Butch?"

"I dropped my stuff and laid right down in the grass, that's what I done. Laid there an hour or more till I figured those Injuns was long gone. But what I figured, too, was that they was prob'ly going over to the wagon road to see if they could find some emigrants to beg or steal from, or even kill if they got the chance. That's what I figured. So when I did come to the road I didn't go out on it. Never did. The whole time I was walking, I just took it for granted there'd be Injuns watching the road too.

"And one man alone, I'd've been easy to pick as an apple in October. I didn't want that, so I held parallel to the road but never ventured out to where an Injun would be sure to see if there was any lurking about. I followed the road on back to post here but didn't ever actually set foot onto it until I was right over there"—he pointed off to the north, toward where the public road passed by Camp Horan on its way west—"and then I hustled across quick as I could lug all that miserable, heavy damned gear." Butch shook his head again. "I tell you, if I had to do it over I'm not sure I wouldn't have just dumped my saddle and claim to've lost it. Not the Spencer, of course. A man would need his gun if it came to a scrap. But that saddle I just might. No use for such as that when some son of a bitch makes you walk like that corporal made me do."

"They'd make you pay for it if you lost your saddle, don't you know," Trooper John Smith reminded.

"After three days carrying the damn thing, I'm not so sure it wouldn't be worth it."

"You want a beer, Butch?"

He grinned. "Bub, I'd carry that saddle three more days for a beer."

"You haven't heard? One of those plain-leg walks-a-heap soldiers told me that one of the civilian wagons passing through this morning delivered two hogsheads of St. Louis beer to Mr. Erickson."

-"Well hell, boys, anybody got any money left over from payday?"

"I do."

"So do I. A little," Donovan reluctantly admitted. In truth, he had nearly all his pay still in his pocket. The other fellows had quickly blown theirs rutting with the laundresses or getting themselves drunk. Donovan hadn't been keen on either of those ideas, so he still had the lion's share of his first pay.

"Hell, then let's go get us some beer quick before all those damn infantry crumbs soak it up."

The barracks, still so new it smelled of sap and sawdust, quickly emptied as the prospect of real, actual, froth and foamy beer allowed the troopers to forget the fatigue of a ten-day patrol.

As bearers of money and other glad prospects, Donovan and the man from Three Squad who'd also admitted to having coins in hand—his name was Albert some-thing-or-other—were given pride of place at the head of the stampede.

Chapter Twenty-three

"Y'know," Donovan mused aloud, "I almost miss cutting and hauling wood." The comment was as much an excuse to pause in the boringly repetitious detail of grooming his horse as it was to convey any sort of information. He plucked an accumulation of loose hair off the hard rubber currycomb and sneezed at the resulting dust—dandruff, more likely—that puffed into the still air inside the huge stable.

"I expect that's what they sent the infantry out here for," Sims put in. "Gives us more time to patrol."

"Ain't that the awful truth. My butt's so sore I've learned to sleep standing up," Smith said with a grin that belied his own words.

Since the arrival of the infantry company, N Troop had far fewer labor details and a corresponding increase in the roving patrols that were intended to keep track of the movement of the Plains tribes and to protect travelers on the Smoky Hill Road from depredations.

Donovan thought about that and with a half-smile said, "We must be doing one helluva job, though, boys. The Indians are so scared of us, we never see any of 'em."

"Not even the ones that're shooting at us," Sims said.

"Why, it's been more'n a week since any done that," Smith reminded them. "And then it was only infantry they was shooting at. No harm done there even if they was t' hit somebody."

Donovan shuddered. He could remember all too clearly the sound of those bullets passing by. It was not a fit subject for humor, he thought. Not even if it was "only" a squad of infantry that had been shot at from afar lately. Of course they *were* only those annoying damned walks-a-heap soldiers. "Any idea who the plainlegs are putting on the line Sunday?" he asked.

"Nope. Haven't heard."

"Some guy named Ezra," Smith said. "That's what I heard anyhow."

"Have you seen him?"

Smith shook his head. Donovan raised his voice so the whole of Four Squad could hear, and maybe some of the others of the troop too. "Anybody gotten a look at this Ezra guy the so'jer boys are running on Sunday?"

Donovan had no idea exactly how the arrangement had come about, but somehow it had been determined that there would be a series of contests between the cavalry and infantrymen on Sunday afternoons. Last week it had been wrestling, and in truth the N Troop gladiator hadn't had a prayer of winning.

It hadn't been anything like fair, most of the troopers concluded. After all, most of the damned plainlegs stood a head taller than any of the cavalrymen, the infantry taking in just about any old trash they could lure into an enlistment but the cavalry accepting only the very best of the best. At least that was their way of looking at the difference. They were also aware, if not particularly interested in bragging about it, that a cavalryman's weight could be absolutely no greater than one hundred forty pounds. And one hundred twenty or less was considered ideal.

The reasoning for this was to limit the amount of total weight that would be carried by a horse. And what with saddle, rations, weapons, and all, there was only so much weight allowance left over to waste on the trooper. Romantic notions aside, cavalrymen were generally small. Tough as nails, the troopers themselves bragged, but undeniably small. And last Sunday's wrestling match had pitted a hundred and thirty-five-pound trooper from Two Squad against a hulking menace of an infantryman who must have weighed well over two hundred pounds and not an ounce of it fat. It hadn't even been a contest, really. But this Sunday it would be foot racing. And John Donovan had some ideas about that.

"If anybody finds out anything about that Ezra guy, how about letting me know?" he asked.

Sims gave him a close look-over. "You thinking about going to the line yourself, John?"

Donovan only shrugged.

But yeah. He was thinking exactly that.

He used to . . . well, that didn't much matter. Not now it didn't. Not here. But he used to run a little. Maybe more than a little.

Yeah, he was thinking about it, all right. But he surely would like to know more about this Ezra soldier before he went and actually said anything about it.

Chapter Twenty-four

Donovan wasn't all that happy about his footwear. Boots, of course, were out of the question. What he really needed was a pair of soft, supple running shoes like those he'd had back home.

Except shoes like that weren't easily come by—especially out here in the middle of absolutely nothing like Camp Horan was. If he only had some proper shoes . . .

But he didn't, and that was that.

Still, he thought, he'd go out there and run.

He'd gotten a glimpse of this Ezra fellow yesterday after evening stables. He'd been pointed out to Donovan by another of the boys from N Troop. Ezra didn't look so awful fast. He was tall enough, but built with thick pads of muscle, not at all the lean and wiry sort that runs best. He looked like a man who enjoyed athletics, but Donovan guessed his best sports would be wrestling or lacrosse or boxing, something like those. Not running.

If he had some decent shoes . . . He'd just have to settle

for what he did have, which was the pair of ordinary street shoes he'd been wearing the day he'd walked in and enlisted. They were terrible running shoes, but almost anything was better than boots. If it hadn't been for all the low-growing and nearly invisible little prickly cactuses on the prairie, he would have run barefoot. That would have been the next best thing to running shoes.

Still . . . he was going to do it. He checked his hoard of saved money. He had six dollars and eighteen cents. He decided he would wager five of it. He might have been willing to plunge for the whole caboodle, except there was no telling when their next pay would be. It could be two, three months away, or even more.

Not that he was going to lose. Of course not.

He stripped down to just his fatigue trousers, laced his street shoes as tight as he could get them, and sorted five dollars in coin out of the poke where he kept his cash.

He was, he figured, ready.

Donovan felt like nine kinds of fool. There that damned Ezra Bittermann stood. Tall and athletic and, damn him, wearing a pair of expensively crafted genuine running shoes, far and away the nicest Donovan had ever laid eyes on. The damned infantryman was a ringer. This fellow obviously knew how to run.

Donovan barely bothered paying attention when the infantry company's top sergeant named off the course and rules for the seven men—three cav and four infantry—who were on the line.

The runners were instructed to start at the north end of the parade ground and run counterclockwise three times around, everyone in full view at all times and nobody to come inside of the oval of white marker pegs or he'd be disqualified. At each of the four turning points there was both an infantryman and someone representing N Troop, all of the judges noncoms of the rank corporal or higher. Most of them, in fact, were three-stripers. Donovan got the idea that rank came easy in the infantry, because all their judges were buck sergeants while only one of the cavalrymen was.

That was no particular disappointment. But Ezra Bittermann sure was. Damn him. With shoes like that, he had to be an accomplished runner. And Donovan was far out of shape. He wished now he hadn't laid so much money on himself.

Too late to back out now, of course. He was already at the line before he noticed Bittermann's shoes, so even if he claimed illness or a cramp at this point, he'd be considered a runner and lose his bet.

But he wished he hadn't been quite so confident.

Nothing to it now but to go ahead and try to keep from making a complete fool of himself.

He cleared his throat and spat. His mouth was dry and he would have liked a swallow of water, but he knew better than to burden himself with a full belly, especially something as heavy as water. All he'd had today was half a cup of coffee and one hard biscuit, and he'd had those a good six hours earlier. The running would be easier on an empty belly. Empty, that is, save for the acid that churned and rumbled as a case of nerves and disappointment set in.

Dang that Bittermann anyway.

"Is everybody clear now? Three times around the course." The grizzled old infantry sergeant grinned. "Anybody wants to stop and rest between laps is welcome to."

The boys who were gathered to watch got a chuckle

out of that, but Donovan noticed that not a single runner so much as smiled.

"To the mark now." The sergeant raised a small pistol and cocked it. "Ready."

Donovan leaped at the squeeze of the sergeant's finger, knowing better than to wait for the sound of the report.

Chapter Twenty-five

That darn Bittermann hadn't looked much like a runner, but he sure enough was one. Son of a gun ran like he didn't know what fatigue was. He started out fast, and he stayed fast. Nobody ought to have wind like that, but Bittermann sure did.

And as good a start as Donovan got, Bittermann got an even better one. He was off like a jackass rabbit right from that opening puff of smoke from the sergeant's pistol, and all Donovan could do was tuck in behind him.

The others, infantry and cav alike, might as well have gone back to their bunks for all the good they were going to do. They were all outdistanced by the time Bittermann reached the first turn, and by the end of the first lap Donovan couldn't even hear them huffing and chuffing back there.

About all he really could hear was the soft sound of Bittermann's shoes hitting the ground and the heavier thump as his own followed.

Donovan stayed on Bittermann's heels. Barely. But his breathing was already difficult, for he was pushing himself.

Three laps. It was a big parade ground, laid out long. Three laps would be . . . what? . . . more than a mile. He wasn't sure how much more. A long enough run to separate the men from the boys, that was sure.

The problem was that from here on the dang infantry would be able to call him "boy" if he couldn't do any better than this.

His feet hurt, his chest ached, and there was a burning sensation in his throat and lungs.

His thighs were starting to feel as if they'd been cased inside thin sheets of flexible lead.

And that damned Bittermann was running as easy and fluid as if . . . Fluid. That was the problem, dammit. Bittermann was running like liquid flowing out of a jar. Donovan was flailing along behind like this was a sprint and not the distance run that it really was.

Bittermann had gotten him right at the start, Donovan realized now. With his own speed off the line Bittermann had suckered Donovan—well, all of them; there wasn't any way Bittermann could have anticipated who among the others might be a real runner and who not—suckered them into that sprint for the first turn.

That was where Donovan made his mistake. He should have taken his time about getting his own stride. Obviously Bittermann had the ability to do that from a spring. Donovan didn't. Never had. This race wouldn't have been any different even if he'd been in shape. Except if he'd been in shape, if he'd been used to running again, then maybe . . . no, surely . . . he would have thought to control his own start and not let Bittermann force him like that.

Too late now, though. A lap and a quarter, nearly half the race, gone and it was all Donovan could do to stay close.

The rest of the boys . . . Donovan couldn't hear their footfalls now, never mind their breathing. They might as well not have been back there, for all the chance they had.

Donovan might as well not be running for all the chance he had, either. Not without his stride, he couldn't. Not without finding that magical, effortless, floating stride of the distance run.

And the really awful thing was that Donovan's stride was much faster than that damn Bittermann's. When he had it. Which he didn't.

"Go, John."

"That's it. Hang with him. You'll nip him at the end."

He could hear the boys shouting encouragement. Their support, oddly, had the opposite effect.

They couldn't see it, no one could from the sidelines, but he knew. He was lost. Bittermann was running fluid and easy. Donovan was not. The burning in his chest and legs would only get worse, and by the final lap Bittermann would run clean away from him.

"Cavalry. Cavalry. Cavalry." The shouts were shrill and eager.

"Infantry. Infantry. Infantry." Bittermann's supporters were equally enthusiastic.

God. How much money had been laid between cavalry and infantry today? A good many of the bets were placed that way. He knew that much.

And even though he still slogged along there just back of Bittermann's shoulder, Donovan knew that his race was as good as lost. No way he could hold this pace for another lap and a half. No way.

Bittermann had beat him there at the start when he had

got out so quick and threw Donovan off his floating stride by making him sprint too hard to that first damn turn.

Without his floating stride he hadn't a prayer, and the only way to get it now would be . . .

"Damn," Donovan groaned half out loud.

With a great whoosh of exhalation and no hope whatsoever, John Donovan stopped dead on the track and gulped for air while Ezra Bittermann sprinted doggedly on down the parade ground course.

Chapter Twenty-six

"Jesus, John, if you weren't about the stupidest-looking thing I ever saw out there. Standing there like that while that infantry guy was running out ahead and the rest of the bunch chasing up behind and getting closer. Then leaping like you'd lost your damn mind. You looked like a big-ass goose, or one of those long-neck wading birds with the skinny legs."

"You looked like you were trying to jump over a bunch of mud puddles. Wasn't like any kind of running I ever seen," Trooper John Smith said with a shake of his head, but with something of a sparkle in his eye, too. Smith had a tin mug of beer in his hand. So did the rest of the boys.

Well, for that matter, so did John Donovan. And he believed he was entitled to it.

He grinned. "I wasn't running fast, boys, because I was trying too hard. Pumping my legs, see, but not stretching them out. And tired as I already was, I had to do something to get into my stride. Only way I could do that was to stop the way I was doing it and start over."

"I never saw anything like it, though," Sims said. "Time you got started again, John, Bittermann was twenty-five, thirty yards in front of you."

"Yes, and he'd have been that far ahead of me at the end, too, if I'd kept on the way I started. The only chance I had . . . only chance the troop had . . . was for me to quit lumbering about like a bear on its hind legs and get into a float. That's what all that bounding was about. Had to get my stride stretched out long and smooth." His grin was fueled by a deep draft of the St. Louis beer. God, it was good. The taste was clean, crisp, and fine, just fine.

"I swear though I never seen anything like it," one of the fellows from One Squad said.

"At the end there that infantry guy looked red as a crabapple in spice. He couldn't believe you was beating him so bad."

"Made him look foolish."

One of the other boys laughed loudly and gleefully. "Made another payday for us, though. I mean, who the hell would've thought it."

Not me, Donovan felt like saying. But didn't. It might have spoiled some of the fun the boys were having. Better to let them think it'd all been slick and easy.

The truth was that Donovan's legs still felt like twice-cooked noodles, and there was still a deep, nagging ache in his chest.

He was pleased enough, though. Bittermann had the fancy shoes and apparently the experience to go with them.

But it was John Donovan and the boys of N Troop who were having the celebration, and that was good. Mighty good.

"Have another beer, John," Louie Gordon offered. "On me."

It occurred to Donovan that tonight he felt completely a part of his four, of the squad, of the troop.

"Let's all have another," he responded with joy.

Chapter Twenty-seven

He really should have been feeling atop the world. After all, he was something of a personage now, if not exactly a hero. Certainly, all the boys of N Troop knew him, and favorably, and if they might have somewhat less regard for him, then at the very least the infantrymen of K Company of the 312th Infantry Regiment also knew who he was. Yessir, Trooper John Donovan was a bona fide, sure enough personage at Camp Horan now, and he really should be feeling on top of the world.

What he did feel was . . . bilious. His stomach felt as if it might never again admit food without protest, and his head pounded most abominably a full day after the Sunday footrace and the celebrations that followed.

Breakfast on this miserable Monday had been coffee and loud groans. At lunch he'd tried, he really had, to eat something. He'd gone through the line and taken his plate—real plates they were now, too, not the mess-kit halves they'd been using ever since the camp was first established—and sat down at one of the newly constructed tables with every intention of eating. A man did, after all, have to eat. It was necessary. But . . . not today. The sight of the runny beans and barely cooked salt pork roiled his stomach and got the gases moving in both directions, and in the end his good intentions came to naught. He passed his plate to Sims to share out among the others of their four and made a hasty exit from the mess hall.

Now, at the sharp, brassy sound of mess call, his stomach lurched and grumbled again.

A taste, a look, the merest *smell* of supper would double him over and set him to spewing. If he had anything left in him to lose, that is, which was doubtful of itself. But still . . .

"Come on, Donovan. Don't wanta be late or the cooks will give it all away before we get there."

"You go ahead, Louie. I don't much feel up to it."

Gordon gave him a laugh and a knowing grin and trotted off with the others of the troop to collect their evening meal.

Donovan remained for a moment on the parade ground where they'd just broken formation. The solitude was pleasant. So was the memory of the race.

He ran it again in his mind, each lap so clearly remembered, then turned. There wasn't another soul in sight at the moment. Cavalry and infantry alike had disappeared into their respective mess halls. And the officers were almost never seen anyway. They had their own quarters and their own pursuits and rarely had any actual contact with the men they purportedly led.

Silence and solitude were a marvel and a rarity, he realized now. He hadn't consciously missed them, but now that they were upon him he discovered that being

93

alone was far from the same thing as being lonely. He quite liked it for a change.

With no temptation to visit the mess hall whatsoever, he ambled, hands in pockets, out to the stables, where the horses had all been fed, groomed, and bedded for the night. Handsome was munching with seeming contentment. Donovan fussed with the ugly horse's headstall, quite unnecessarily checked his tie rope, and gave the horse an extra fork of the timothy hay that had been hauled in from God-knew-where by a civilian contractor.

When he left the stables he turned on a whim, not back toward camp with its bustle and noise and the smell of so many men, but west, toward the creek and a now silent copse of woods that someone had ordered exempt from the woodcutting, perhaps for reasons of aesthetics or possibly from some more utilitarian reasoning that escaped Donovan's understanding.

However the stand of trees came under that protection, they were pretty in their mantle of bright, pale spring green. Their quiet beckoned. And he had, after all, hours yet before the sounding of tattoo.

It occurred to him about halfway to the woods that there was always the possibility that a hostile might be lurking there, eager to waylay and scalp a soldier so foolishly unwary as to wander alone to the creek.

But then, it had been some time since any of the red men had sniped at the woodcutters. And he didn't believe any of them had ever ventured so close to the camp itself. Generally the hostiles preferred to lie out on the prairie, hidden in the grasses near the top of one of the countless, barely discernible, rises that rolled and undulated for miles in every direction.

He was probably safe enough.
Probably.
But he walked the rest of the way a little more slowly
and with his eyes more widely opened.

Chapter Twenty-eight

Oh, God. He shouldn't have come out here. Why had he been so stupid?

He felt the creepy-crawly prickle of fear tingling at the nape of his neck, and his stomach felt hollow and fluttery. He was sure his hair was standing up just like on a feist dog when another, bigger dog comes around.

Indians. He was sure of it.

Well, almost sure of it.

He was alone out here beside the creek. Completely alone in a patch of quiet woods. He'd *thought* he was alone, anyway.

Except now he'd heard footfalls. Soft, slow, almost silent footfalls. Moving ever so slowly, ever so quietly toward the log he was sitting on.

Donovan's first thought was flight. He desperately wanted to jump up, whirl, run like hell toward Camp Horan.

But fleet as he might be, the fastest man on the post, no one was fast enough to outrace an arrow or a bullet.

If he moved . . . did the Indians even know he was here? Perhaps they didn't. Perhaps his own movement would give him away if he jumped and ran. Perhaps . . . if it wasn't him they were sneaking toward but a place from which they could fire randomly at soldiers moving in the distance . . . perhaps he still had a chance.

If he could hide . . . if he could just manage to avoid them . . . he might yet survive.

He would lie here the whole night through if that was what it took. Let them call tattoo back at quarters. Let them signal taps. Would someone look for him if he failed to show up? Mmm, not likely. They would think he'd deserted. Some did. It wasn't unknown. If they thought he'd taken his winnings from the race and run off, they wouldn't bother to come after him until tomorrow. Tomorrow he could well be dead.

But if the Indians didn't know he was here. . . .

He heard another of the slow but continuing hints of noise and motion from off to his right, from upstream along the creek.

Steeling his nerve against a desire to freeze, to make no sound whatsoever, he slid carefully backward, bracing himself on the rough bark of the fallen log and inching silently over the log and down.

He stretched full length onto the ground, every crunch or crackle of a dead leaf striking fear into his belly as he hid close beside the fallen tree and tucked tight against it.

He breathed carefully, trying not to make any noise that could give him away. None. The ground smelled of loam and mold and decay, although not unpleasantly so. Under the circumstances, the scent seemed comforting and rather nice.

The wild pounding of his heart could probably be heard a dozen feet distant, he thought. Certainly he could hear it loud and plain in his ears. He willed the mad beating to slow, but it did not.

The sounds came nearer and more easily distinguished above the faint and gentle burble of moving water.

The Indians were close now, between his log and the water. Moving right to left, but slowly. So slowly. Donovan had to force back an impulse to throw up. Or to shriek and bolt toward the camp, toward safety.

A cold, empty tingle developed in the small of his back, right where an arrow or a bullet might take him if he tried now to run. The hair on top of his head felt tight as a too-small knitted cap as it contracted and prickled. Wild Indians took scalps. And worse. He'd seen it. Oh Lord, he had truly seen it for himself that day out on the road.

If it had to happen, then please, please God let him be dead before they did all those awful things to him. Before they cut off his hair and . . . those other even more terrible things that they did.

He had to stay here. He had to hope they wouldn't see him, wouldn't hear him.

But when it happened, if it happened, he hoped he would not disgrace himself. He hoped he could die like a man and not a sniveling mole.

Perhaps he should stand up. Face them brave and defiant and proud. Except, oh dear God, he didn't want to die. He didn't.

Oh, God, he . . .

"Damn!"

Donovan gasped. Out loud.

Indians . . . surely Indians didn't cuss in English. And the voice . . .

He raised himself off the ground, and peeped over the rubbed and peeling bark on top of the log.

It wasn't an Indian he saw standing beside the creek.

It was a woman. A *white* woman.

"Damn," she muttered again, and he saw that she'd stepped in mud where some fluctuation of the creek level had left a puddle.

Donovan felt a mingling of great and satisfying relief, but also shame and embarrassment as he considered whether to show himself to the woman or stay hidden where he was.

Really he should play the gentleman, he supposed, and offer to clean her shoe or something. On the other hand, a lady wasn't supposed to know words like that, much less use them, and it might be uncomfortable for her to know her exclamation had been overheard.

No, he probably should just stay where he was, let the lady pass on by, never knowing she'd been observed. That was really the better thing to do. He was sure of it. He could just let her go on down the stream and when she was well out of sight and hearing he would go back to the camp and . . .

His hand, bracing himself on the log, slipped when a slab of loose bark gave way. He fell, the side of his chest slamming quite painfully onto the unyielding wood, driving the breath from him and wrenching from his lips a sharp "damn" of his own to match those of the lady.

So much for staying in hiding.

The woman turned, startled, and Donovan gave her a weak and apologetic smile.

He felt as if he'd deliberately set out to spy on her and now was caught at it.

He hadn't done any such thing, of course. But he doubted he could expect her to believe that.

Damn, he said again, but this time only to himself.

With a sigh he rose from behind the log, brushed his hands together, and dusted bits of broken leaves and forest litter off his shirt and trousers. Then, ready to take his medicine of scorn—preferable to an arrow in the back, anyway—he stepped over the log and marched resolutely forward.

Chapter Twenty-nine

"Are you all right, miss? Can I help?" The term "miss" was a courtesy, pure and simple. This was no girl. He could see that as he approached her. She was probably in her thirties, he guessed. Which meant she would not only be married, she'd likely have a small herd of children, and perhaps some of them already grown or mostly so. It was common enough for a woman to have grandbabies by the time she was halfway through her thirties.

"Where did you . . . ?"

He gave her a reassuring smile. "I was sitting on that log over there." He pointed with his chin. And he wasn't lying, exactly. He had indeed been sitting on the log— right up until he'd hid behind it. "I'm in the cavalry, miss. Over there at the fort." Again he pointed, then regretted the gesture. It wasn't like someone was very much apt not to notice there was an army fort in plain sight a couple hundred yards away. "You must've come in on a train,

I expect," he said. "I didn't notice there was wagons fresh in. My name is John Donovan." He remembered, a little late, that he had his hat on and quickly plucked it off so as to correct that breach of manners.

The woman hesitated a moment—frightened to be alone in the company of a man she didn't know, perhaps—then mumbled something that he didn't quite hear. In a slightly stronger voice she added, "My name is Sarah." She didn't give a last name. But then, he thought, it could be she didn't want him to say anything to her husband about finding her here.

Not that a lowly private soldier like Trooper Donovan was likely to be introduced to any of the emigrants passing through, male or female. This woman right here was the first he'd ever spoken to. He'd buried some, of course, and seen others going by. But a common soldier didn't socialize with proper folk. Common soldiers, he was discovering, were beneath the station of even the poorest of emigrants. Or so the emigrants themselves seemed to view things.

"I . . . can I help you?" he asked again, looking down. Which was the direction his eyes had taken anyway, as he got to thinking about his current place as opposed to that of a lady.

She'd stepped in that puddle, all right, and she'd gotten more than a muddy shoe. She'd gone and lost her shoe entirely, it being still there in the grip of the sticky, clinging clay that made up the creek bank. The woman, Sarah, was standing with one shoe on and the other covered only by a rough stocking.

Donovan knelt quickly and pulled the shoe free. Darn thing was stuck in there pretty good and he had to give it a hard pull, but he did manage to get it loose.

He was kneeling so close beside the woman that he could smell the faint, yeasty scent of her coming off her skirts, and that bothered him. He tried to ignore it.

"This is awful muddy, miss. Let me wash it off for you."

"No, don't bother."

"It's no bother, miss."

"No, it's . . . Please don't wash it. The sole has cardboard patches inside. Please don't wet it."

"Yes, miss. I'll just . . . kinda . . . scrape some of the mud off. Are you all right for another minute? D'you want me to carry you over to that log?" The thought of picking her up, holding her in his arms—never mind that she was a married lady and all—was bothersome too. But in an entirely different way.

"I'm fine like this, thank you."

Of course she was. Of course. He felt foolish for having asked. But he would have been pleased had she accepted. He looked about on the ground, found a twig that was stout enough, and quickly scraped some of the worst of the mud away from the shoe.

He could see now why it had come off so easily. It wasn't tied. Not a fancy dress-up slipper, it was a real shoe and should have been securely tied, but the laces were rotten and broken and patched so small that they only held together the lowest couple of eyelet pairs. "Do you want . . . d'you want me to see if I can find some twine or something to hold this on better the next time?" he suggested.

"No. Please. Just help me put it back on, please."

She lifted her stockinged leg and wobbled just a little as she balanced on one limb. Incredibly, she reached down to touch Donovan's shoulder to steady herself and with her other hand lifted her skirt several inches to give him better access to her foot.

He could see her ankle and half her calf, and now that she was so near the scent of her was almost overpowering. He felt a stirring, an urge, that was familiar and frightening and bothersome and . . .

"Trooper Donovan?"

"Oh, I . . . sorry, ma'am. Miss. I'm sorry." Hastily he positioned the shoe beneath her foot. Then hesitated. Swallowed. There seemed no other way to do it, really. Reluctantly but with a tingle of anticipation he placed his free hand behind her heel, the warmth of her flesh biting hot even with the cloth of the stocking between his skin and hers, and rather awkwardly wiggled and shoved and pushed to get the errant shoe back onto her foot.

He managed to muddy himself more than a little in the process.

But he didn't regret it. Oh no, he did not.

He could feel the burn of twin furnaces in his ears as he reacted to the sight of a practically naked foot and ankle and calf and the other warm and very heady sensations he was experiencing.

"Are you all right?" she asked, obviously noticing his difficulty.

"Yeah, I'm . . . I'm fine, miss. And you?"

"Fine, thank you." She paused. "Trooper."

"Yes, ma'am? Miss?"

"Would you please let my foot down now?"

His ears turned even hotter, and the heat spread instantly onto his cheeks and across his forehead. He ducked his head and turned half away, knowing that it was too late for that but making the effort anyway.

He also remembered—finally—to let go of the woman's foot.

She removed her hand from his shoulder and straightened.

Donovan stood. The woman, Sarah, was tall—taller than he by several inches. Now that they were standing face-to-face, and she was slightly higher than he on the creek bank, he had to tip his head back and look up to see her.

She had a careworn face, he thought. She'd not had an easy life of it. But then, how many in this world ever do. Her hair, a dark and rather lifeless brown, was pulled into a severe bun, the tug of it drawing the skin tight at her temples.

She was not pretty really, although she might have been when she was a girl. He could imagine her face younger and smoother, without the ravages of time and labor, and she might have been very pretty then.

As it was, she still had very pretty eyes. He liked her eyes. They were multihued, with flecks of gold and green and gray and brown. He wasn't exactly sure what one would call eyes that color, but they were pretty. Younger than the rest of her, he thought, and filled with calm, with intelligence. Yes, she had good eyes.

She also . . . he shouldn't have noticed but could not help doing so . . . she also had a very generous mouth and lips. Not thin and hard, as he would have expected on a woman of her age, but soft and, well, puffy.

He noticed them. Felt the return of heat to his face. Looked quickly away. Very quickly.

"You're all right now, miss?"

"I'm fine, thank you."

"Would you . . . uh . . . d'you want me to walk you back to your wagons?"

"No." Her voice was soft, and he thought there was the sound of a smile in it, but he did not want to look back at her again to see if he was right. "I'll look where I'm walking from now on and avoid the mud. But I thank you, Trooper Donovan." He heard the tiny, furry sound of a poorly contained chuckle, and she said, "You've been a great help to me this evening, Trooper. More so than you will ever know."

"I . . . I'm glad, ma'am. Miss."

"Good-bye, John."

His first name. He found it quite incredible that she would have called him by his first name.

He felt a touch on his elbow, so light he wasn't sure he felt it at all.

And then she was gone. He heard the soft footsteps—not Indians but a woman named Sarah—and when he turned again to look she was gone, disappeared into the trees somewhere.

It was coming dusk and the light was failing. It was time for him to head back to the barracks anyway.

He felt better now than he had, though. Indeed, he felt quite good. Even his stomach was less troubling, and he suspected that by breakfast he would be ready to eat enough for the entire four—heck, enough for the squad.

Donovan found himself smiling as he walked back across the prairie toward Camp Horan, and under his breath he whistled a gay tune.

Chapter Thirty

"Are you as sore as I am?" Sims groaned.

"Not me. I could keep on riding till old Handsome's legs wear down to his knees." Now that was a lie, sure enough. The truth was that his backside ached, his thighs were so sore they quivered and twitched, his knees hurt, and his head throbbed—although what that had to do with sitting on a dang horse for day after day after day he hadn't yet figured out. He was altogether miserable.

But it wasn't going to do any good to complain about a single bit of it, so why bother.

"Well, I'm sore," Sims grumbled.

Donovan turned his head and grinned at Sims, who was riding beside him in the loose column of twos they traveled in when on mounted patrol. "Don't you worry, Ed. Won't be long and we'll trot again."

Almost as if he'd heard and was agreeably responding, up at the front of the small column the lieutenant called for the trot. The sergeant repeated the order—as if the lieutenant were too far above them to deign speaking directly to his troopers, so everything he said had to be repeated—and more or less in unison the patrol squeezed their mounts into the trot.

Forty minutes at the walk. Ten minutes at the trot. Ten minutes dismounted and leading the horses. That was the normal way of things unless they were in active pursuit of hostiles—which Donovan had never once experienced, although he'd heard some of the other fellows talk about it—or were on a quick march.

In front of him Louie Gordon moaned loudly enough for the whole rest of the squad to hear. Not because of the jostling of the trot. They were all accustomed to that and had been thoroughly taught to take the pounding with their knees and not bang down on the saddle, so as not to hurt the horses. It also made the trot easier to sit once a fellow got used to it, and none of them really minded proceeding at a trot. Louie's problem was when they were ordered to dismount and walk for the ten minutes. Louie had boots a size or more too small, and they hurt his feet something fierce. As he informed every- and anyone within hearing on every occasion possible.

Donovan gave Handsome his head, letting the horse maintain their place in the column while he peered off toward the distance.

There were clouds building out to the west, so high and white and handsome that they looked like mountain peaks. Pretty, he thought, and wondered if someday he would see a real mountain.

Back east they talked about the west like it was all mountains—huge, rocky, and capped with snow the whole year round.

There might well be such mountains. Donovan wouldn't know about that. But he could sure enough attest that they didn't occupy *all* the west. He'd been out here for months now, and about all he'd seen was grass, grass, and then some more grass. Grass and dust, that is. You wouldn't think there could be so much dust raised when the ground was covered with grass, but there was dust enough and then some.

He got a whiff of it up his nose as the horses ahead of him—and why was Four Squad always at the back end of the column, anyway?—raised it out of the thick but already browning prairie grass. He sneezed and felt his nose begin to run, so he ran the sleeve of his blouse across his mouth and upper lip to wipe away snot and dust and grime.

The lieutenant veered right without warning; and Donovan, his horse blindly following where the others led, was caught unprepared and swayed precariously atop the hard, skinny McClellan saddle. He righted himself and rose up a little in his stirrups to look ahead and see what it was that had caught the lieutenant's interest up there.

He felt his heartbeat quicken.

Indians. There were Indians.

Maybe some of the murderous raiders who'd been marauding along the road of late. Maybe some of the very ones who'd killed those poor emigrant folks earlier in the spring.

Donovan reached down and touched the wrist and action of the Spencer carbine that lay muzzle down in the leather socket attached to the side of his saddle.

It was Smith's turn today to hold the horses for their four if they went into dismounted action, and Donovan felt a flash of satisfaction. If they got into a fight he would be able to give something back for those dead folks.

"At the gallop," the lieutenant called out, the order repeated instantly by the sergeant. "Ho!"

Donovan tugged his hat more tightly onto his head and settled into the saddle. He didn't have to prod Handsome to keep up. As soon as the other horses broke from the trot, Handsome did too, laying its ears flat in a show of mild pique but responding so as to hold its place.

"Now, what I can't remember," Ed Sims said with a grin, "is whether I brought along any ca'tridges for this here rifle gun."

"I left mine back to camp," Gordon said to no one in particular. "Too damn heavy to carry."

"You can have one of mine, Louie," Donovan put in, getting into the spirit of it. "I brought two."

"Hell, we're all right, then."

The Indians weren't half a mile away, encamped in a shallow swale where their conical tents hadn't been visible until the patrol was almost upon them.

With the cavalry coming down at them it was like someone had kicked an anthill. Indians were scurrying and running in all directions at once, dashing every which way, and none of it making any apparent sense.

"At the trot, boys. Now at the walk. Squads abreast." The sergeant's voice came so close on the lieutenant's commands as to seem an echo rather than a separate sound.

"Carbines at the ready."

Donovan felt an emptiness in the pit of his stomach as he reached to drag the heavy Spencer from its keeper and hold it muzzle upright, the buttplate resting on his right thigh.

There were ... he didn't know how many Indians. Scores of them. But some were women and some were kids and a whole, awful lot of them were men. Warriors. With rifles and bows.

The women and the kids ducked into the tents— lodges, he'd been told they were called, not tents, but they sure as hell looked like tents to him—and now there were only the men in sight. Scores of them.

There were, what, twenty-some guys in the patrol.

The Indians saw them and stood in a bunch—waiting, Donovan supposed—but they weren't shooting. Not yet, anyhow. And the lieutenant wasn't saying anything about preparing to charge.

Not yet, anyhow.

Donovan felt cold in the middle, although it was a plenty warm enough day.

He felt cold and sick and breathless and God knew what else.

"Patrol, halt."

The sergeant didn't need to repeat that one, and every horse in the line was yanked to a stop in half the time they would have managed on the parade ground back at Horan.

"Stand at the ready."

Donovan felt a lump in his throat that he couldn't swallow out of the way. His mouth was dry and his hands so sweaty he was afraid he would drop his dang carbine.

Louie Gordon on his left and Ed Sims on his right looked calm and cool as stones in a stream. Donovan felt ashamed of himself for the cold fear that flashed through his gut, felt ashamed of it but unable to quell it or make it go away. The best he could do, the very best, was to sit

111

there where he was told and hold on to the Spencer and his reins like he ought to and wait. And if the order came, well, he'd do his best and hope he didn't shame himself or let the other boys down, that was all.

Chapter Thirty-one

Now he knew why they paid lieutenants so much more than a common soldier drew. Lieutenant Harmon was in the middle of the line with Sergeant Pfeiffer and Tom Albrecht, the guidon bearer. The lieutenant said something to Pfeiffer and then to Albrecht, then bumped his horse into a slow lope.

Pfeiffer stayed where he was, but darned if Albrecht didn't have to go along with the lieutenant as they left the protection of the patrol behind and rode forward alone to talk with the Indians.

Albrecht, who'd earned the honor of carrying the guidon by way of being hopelessly inept with the handling of weapons—he was impossibly clumsy even with the sabers that were now some scores of miles away back in barracks—was *not* earning extra pay to be out there where the Indians could get at him easy if the talking didn't go well.

The lieutenant rode out like he hadn't a nerve in his body, and poor old Albrecht stayed level with the rump of the officer's privately owned and almighty handsome bay gelding.

The two of them rode smack up to the Indians, who were bunched up together and not spread out into anything that looked like a fighting formation. Rode so close they could talk without raising their voices and where it would have been nigh impossible for the hostiles to miss their aim if talking didn't work and they turned to shooting.

That was brave, Donovan thought. Awful brave of them both.

Even from the distance of sixty or seventy yards back, Donovan could see how nervous Albrecht was. The rider's worries were transmitted to his horse, and the animal was skittish, shifting its weight from side to side, tossing its head, turning its ears this way and that. Albrecht was holding way too tight a rein on it, and the horse didn't like that.

Not that Donovan faulted the guidon bearer. Not in the slightest. If he'd been up there armed with nothing but a long stick and a short pistol, he expected he'd have been sitting on a short rein ready to get the hell outa there in one very large hurry just like Albrecht was.

There was some movement among the Indians, and after a bit two of them walked out from the rest of the bunch. They came up right beside the lieutenant's left stirrup and talked. Must have been in English, Donovan supposed, because it was a two-way conversation. Donovan kind of wished he could've heard what was being said. If there'd been a way to do it without getting close, that is. He didn't envy Albrecht for being up there. Nossir, he did not.

Donovan kept looking between the lieutenant out there with the Indians and Sergeant Pfeiffer, who would be the one they'd have to look to for orders if anything got started. The other boys were doing the same, he saw. Pfeiffer had the lieutenant's instructions about what to do. If they had to do something, which Donovan sure as hell hoped they didn't.

The butt of the Spencer was hard and heavy on his leg, and he frequently had to steady it with his rein hand while he wiped the flat of his right hand dry on the cloth of his trousers.

As time and the talking went on, though, he was able to relax and not be quite so tense. The more they talked, the less likely it was that anything was going to happen.

Sure enough, after ten or fifteen minutes the lieutenant reached down and solemnly shook hands with first one of the Indians he'd been parlaying with and then the other.

The Indians turned and said something to the rest of the bunch, and then they relaxed too.

Donovan hadn't consciously realized how tense the crowd of Indian warriors were, but now they were standing easy he could see the difference in them just like he could feel it in himself and all down the line of troopers on either side of him.

Whatever it was that'd been said over there, there wasn't going to be any fighting now.

The two Indians went back to stand with the rest of them, and the lieutenant saluted and did something with his reins and legs to make his bay drop down in the front like a bow or a salute too. Donovan hadn't known the horse could do something like that, but without a doubt the trick was impressive. Spiffy and formal. He could see that the Indians liked it too.

The lieutenant sat tall as he wheeled the bay, Albrecht close on his heels, and rode back to the patrol without so much as a glance in the direction of the Indians.

He stopped facing the patrol, and to Pfeiffer, but loud enough for all of them to hear—deliberately so, Donovan was sure—said, "There is a spring of good water on the other side of that rise, Sergeant. We will bivouac there tonight." And in an even louder and slightly brusque tone, he finished, "Patrol. In column of twos, at the walk, forward . . . ho!"

They rode away like there never had been any worries whatsoever.

But it did occur to Donovan later that the lieutenant didn't have them return their carbines to the keepers. They kept the weapons in hand right up until they were ordered to dismount and begin preparations for another night with nothing but stars and clouds for a roof.

Chapter Thirty-two

It was a rare and relaxing evening. Or would have been except for the knowledge that a tribe of savages was camped little more than a quarter mile distant, on the other side of a knoll. Why the Indians hadn't chosen to place their tents beside the pond that was the only nearby source of water, Donovan did not know. But he was pleased they'd left it alone.

Not that the place was anything special. It was no more than rainwater gathered in a depression. A few stunted cattails suggested that the spot was wet much of the year but not all the time. There were no trees or glades of verdant grasses. Just the bowl-like depression with water in it, and mud all around it, mud that was liberally dotted with the footprints of more kinds of birds and animals large and small than Donovan could begin to recognize.

The thing that made this camp special was that they went into it so early in the day. The normal procedure was for the patrol to continue its wide-ranging sweep until so close to sundown that the troopers' housekeeping duties could not be concluded until well after dark.

This time, the lieutenant obviously wanting for some reason to remain close to the Indian encampment, they had several hours of free time to while away at their leisure.

They set up the iron posts and hemp cable for the picket line, while the horses were allowed the equally unusual pleasure of freely grazing, albeit under close guard.

The men even had time and daylight in which to unroll the seldom-used two-man shelters, each man carrying one canvas half that buttoned together at the peak. Donovan combined his with Ed Sims's, while Louie Gordon and John Smith shared the luxury of camp quarters in their four.

Most wondrous of all, though, was the fact that they had ample daylight in which to scout the ground for dried buffalo dung. That and grass were the only combustibles to be found so far from standing timber, and the boiling of coffee depended on being able to build a fire.

They could manage a meal without fire if they had to. Hardtack soaked in cold water and salty bacon as tough and chewy as rubber, eaten without benefit of cooking, would do if nothing else was possible. But it was coffee, black and stout, that fueled a cavalryman on patrol, and this night they could look forward to all they wanted of it.

As chef du jour for the four, Ed Sims gathered each man's contribution of beans and rice, combining them into a single pot to cook together and dumping a generous measure of crushed coffee beans into another pot. While he was busy with that, Donovan and Gordon collected buffalo chips. Smith was posted among the horse guards. The others would have their turns later.

Before the first pot of coffee was done the Indians began to show up.

Donovan had never seen any of the hostiles close up and never expected to see any in such a peaceful disposition.

The women came first, trudging along often with children in tow, each hand burdened by skin buckets with which to carry water. But then, of course, Donovan recognized when he thought of it, they naturally would have to come here for their water.

He still did not understand why they would choose to camp completely out of sight from the pond and carry water such a distance, but having done so they would have to make the journey several times daily.

Only the women approached to begin with, but he could see some of the men—acting as guards, perhaps?—standing on top of the knoll between the two campsites.

A few of the troopers spoke to the women, but not all their comments were decent, and it bothered Donovan that such things would be said in the presence of small children. He knew that the Indians, grown or small, could not likely understand the words. But still, such language was not seemly, and his ears burned a little on their behalf.

He was fascinated by the sight of them, though. They were . . . people. Dressed differently, of course, in rude garments made of animal skin and blanket pieces. And their clothes were decorated with gaudy glass beads and bits of seashell from some unimaginably distant shore—and however they could have come by those he did not understand—in odd and disquieting designs.

119

The women were not handsome. Not in the slightest. They were dumpy of form and flat of face, and their flesh was not red at all but more a dark, rather rich brown.

But they were . . . people. Rather ordinary people, at that. These Indians did not look frightening or threatening or inhuman. Just . . . different.

They intrigued him. And all the more so after the women finished collecting water—none of them seeming to deign to look directly at the gaping, staring, lewdly talking soldiers who surrounded them—and went back to their own camp.

Because then the men came. A few of them.

Unlike the women, the men came to beg. To demand, really. By ones and twos the warriors, unarmed now except for the rather wicked knives they carried in pouches at their waists, came into the camp and boldly approached the fires where troopers from each of the fours tended the evening meals.

The Indians jabbered in their own heathen tongue but made themselves clear by gesture: reaching out as if plucking food from the fire, rubbing their bellies, and smacking their lips.

"Son of a bitch wants our supper, damn him," Sims said as Donovan dumped another armload of buffalo chips beside the fire.

"You can give him yours if you want, but I want mine my own self," Louie Gordon put in, then he, too, added to their supply of "firewood" for the evening.

"How's that coffee coming?" Donovan asked.

"Weak, but I expect you could have a cup now. Or did you want to give it to the Indian?"

"I'll drink it myself, thanks." Donovan would have killed for a cup of coffee at the moment. Figuratively speaking, that is. He looked at the Indian who was still making hand gestures and felt sort of sorry for him. The Indian probably wasn't into his twenties yet. He was young and skinny and had a really nasty scar on his right cheek. It looked like a burn mark and must have hurt something awful when it happened.

He wore little but a breechclout and those odd-looking skin shoes that the Indians called moccasins. His hair was greasy and braided into a pair of thick ropes, with small feathers stuck somehow into them. He had a leather thong around his neck and a tiny leather bag dangled from that, hanging over a hairless pigeon chest. A larger bag was suspended from the strap that served him for a belt.

And, of course, there was the knife. It looked actually like a perfectly ordinary kitchen knife except for the brass tacks driven in two rows down both sides of the handle. The knife, too, hung at his waist.

Seen up close like this, with no rifle or bow or any of the crazy war paint that everyone talked so much about, the Indian looked sort of . . . pathetic almost.

For a moment Donovan was tempted to give the Indian some of his supper.

But then the Indian said something in a harsh voice and gave Sims a look that had something of a sneer in it, and the impulse died as quickly as it had been born.

"Get away from here, Lo." Sims made a gesture as if shooing a fly away from the table. "Get, damn you." He pointed.

The Indian said something back—judging by the tone of voice, it was probably a good thing none of them could understand what he said—then turned his back in a huff and strode away toward his own camp and his own damned supper.

"The hell with him," Louie said. "Bunch of damn beggars."

All through the camp the others seemed to be finding much the same result. The troopers hadn't food enough with them that they could afford to squander any, because if their rations ran out before the patrol was completed they would simply ride on with empty bellies. And if anyone was going to be hungry, the consensus was that it should be an Indian and not a cavalryman.

"The hell with them," Donovan agreed aloud.

But he sort of wished they did have enough to share.

He put the Indians and their problems out of his mind, though, and crawled inside their shelter to rummage in his saddlebags for a tin cup so he could have some of that coffee.

Lordy, but fresh boiled coffee did smell exceptionally fine out here in the middle of the empty prairie. Yes sir, it most surely did.

Chapter Thirty-three

"What I want to know is how those dang Injuns snuck off like that without none of us suspecting it."

Donovan shook his head. "Damn if I know, Ed. All those tents. Horses. Dogs. Must have been a couple hundred people there, all told. I wouldn't of thought they could pack up and go in the middle of the night like that."

But they'd seen it. With their own eyes they'd seen it. A couple of the troopers from Two Squad were detailed to check on the Indian camp first thing come daybreak, and just about everyone in the patrol had hiked up to the top of the knoll to see for themselves what they claimed about the Indians being gone.

It was true for certain sure. All that was left were some rings in the grass where the lodges had been, the dark circles of cold ash in their firepits, and the mounds of dung, both horse and human, that were scattered here, there, and everywhere.

It was crazy. Donovan—none of them—would have believed it possible for so many people to disassemble an entire village and go away in the middle of the night like that and do it so quietly that the men standing guard duty couldn't hear.

"Are we gonna chase them?" Donovan asked. Not that Ed Sims was privy to the lieutenant's plans any more than he was, but Ed was an experienced soldier and therefore could be expected to know such things.

"I reckon not," Ed said. "They haven't done nothing to make us follow after them."

"How d'you know that?"

Ed grinned. "Because they rode north. I noticed the direction the marks took where they dragged those travois things. They went north sure enough. Now, us, we're going east. Starting the swing back toward camp, I'd guess. And if we aren't following after them, well, it stands to reason that they haven't done nothing to make us interested in them, doesn't it?"

Donovan could not refute the veteran's logic.

Besides, pretty much everyone knew that bands of Indians traveling with their women and their kids weren't on the warpath, so this bunch wasn't the murderous kind.

"What are you smiling at?" Ed asked him.

Donovan blinked. He'd been caught woolgathering and hadn't realized he was smiling, but now that he thought about it he supposed that he was. He grinned and said, "I was just remembering something. Warpath. You know what that is, don't you?"

"Of course. Everybody's heard that term."

"Yeah, well, when I was a kid listening to the stories about Tecumseh and Simon Girty and all of them, I remember how they talked about the Warpath. Warpath this and Warpath that." He chuckled. "I used to think there was an actual, honest-to-Pete road someplace, a path through the woods sort of thing, that was *the* famous, actual, right-there-on-the-ground Warpath. And I used to wonder why the soldiers didn't never think to post guards or something to keep the Indians from following that Warpath road down to the settlements. Kinda ambush 'em before they got anywhere, don't you see."

Sims laughed. "Well, you're older now and a soldier yourself. I guess this is your time to guard the Warpath, isn't it?"

"Yeah. Or the Smoky Hill emigrant road. Whatever."

"Lucky for us, those Indians we saw weren't on your Warpath. It looks like this will be an easy enough patrol." Ed groaned and rolled his eyes. "Except for making my butt sore, that is."

"Shhh!" Donovan cautioned under his breath. Up at the front of Four Squad Corporal Rathburn was turning around and glaring. Of course, a scowl was Rathburn's ordinary facial expression, but in this case Donovan took it as a warning to maintain silence in the ranks. As if the Indians didn't already know there were troopers in the field, or couldn't hear the clank and rattle of all their gear, or, for that matter, couldn't just look and see a couple dozen mounted men moving across the prairie with a red and white guidon leading the way. Yes sir, they'd have to be quiet all right if they intended to sneak up on anybody that way.

Ed Sims saw the direction of Donovan's eyes and hushed. He waited until Rathburn returned his attention to the front of the column and then made a vulgar gesture toward the corporal's back.

Midmorning and it was already awfully hot, Donovan

was thinking. If they were lucky tonight, they would find a stream or large pond to bivouac beside and they could strip off and go for a swim to cool down. Wash some of this dang dust off, too.

Thinking how it would feel to wallow in some cool water took his mind off the heat and off the Indians—how very ordinary they'd seemed, what with their families and pets and everything there in their village.

He stifled a yawn and deliberately encouraged thoughts about a swim while the horses plodded along at the walk.

Chapter Thirty-four

Donovan could hear soft, muted popping somewhere off to the south of their way. It sounded like sticks breaking. Except, of course, there were no trees to provide sticks for the breaking.

It sounded too much like the dull, oddly soft reports made by distant guns back at Camp Horan when the Indians were sniping at the woodcutters or hay mowers.

"Uh-oh," a voice somewhere in the column expressed on behalf of all of them.

"Troop!" It was just a two-squad patrol and not the whole troop, but the lieutenant must have forgotten that minor detail. Certainly there was an edge of eager excitement in the officer's voice.

"Patrol," Sergeant Pfeiffer loudly repeated.

"At the canter."

"At the canter."

"Ho."

"Ho."

The lieutenant veered south off their previous line of march and the column picked up speed, first opening the gap between pairs and then closing tight together as they headed for what surely was gunfire.

Buffalo hunters, Donovan was thinking. Let's hope it's nothing more than buffalo hunters.

Not that they were seeing buffalo in the huge numbers everyone assured him would come later on in the season. He'd seen a few in the distance, but only a few up until now. They said the vast, migrating herds would arrive in their area of responsibility in another month or two, but they hadn't put in their annual appearance quite yet.

"D'you think it could be buffalo hunters?" Donovan asked of no one in particular, not more than a few scant seconds after firmly ordering himself to avoid that foolish question.

"No," Trooper John Smith snapped.

"I wish to hell it was," Ed Sims responded. "But it ain't."

"Quiet in the ranks," Rathburn growled without looking back. He didn't need to. His voice carried to them just fine.

Donovan felt the same fluttering thrill in the hollow of his suddenly empty stomach that he'd felt the other day—two days ago? no, three it had been now—when they'd first seen that Indian village out to the west.

He hoped he didn't do anything to embarrass himself or to let the fellows down.

It took him a moment to remember who was named horse holder for the day. Smith, it was. Donovan wasn't honestly sure if he liked that or if he would have preferred to be the one to stay back and handle all four animals if the squad was ordered to skirmish on foot.

The carbine, was it . . . ? He reached down to touch the breech, then felt the heavy spring clip at the end of the keeper to make sure it was securely attached to the steel ring on the side of the Spencer. Even if he dropped the weapon, he wouldn't lose it. It couldn't fall any farther than to the end of the sashlike leather belting that was slung over his left shoulder and across his chest to the right side of his waist.

A heavy leather pouch on his right hip contained his ammunition. He felt to make sure that was all right there, too. Ten tubes, each holding seven of the stubby, .56-caliber rimfire cartridges. The Spencer loaded and fired quickly, and that was to the good.

Unlike the dreadful muzzle loaders of the recent past, or the sturdy but still very slow single-shot Sharps carbines, the Spencer had a magazine tube embedded in the buttstock of the weapon. All a man had to do to reload was to thumb the buttplate end of the magazine a quarter turn to the right and yank the spring-loaded tube out, upend one of the loaders over it to dump in seven fresh cartridges, and shove the spring mechanism down onto them. Then it was simply crank, cock, and fire until you ran empty and had to do it all over again.

With a carbine like the Spencer, a single squad had just about the same amount of firepower that a whole troop could have produced as recently as during the war.

That was what they told him.

Funny, Donovan thought, how that knowledge did not make him feel the least bit better right now.

"At the gallop."

"At the gallop."

"Ho."

"Ho."

129

The horses surged forward, the gallop turning into a run and the close column deteriorating into a loose mass of men and animals as they approached the source of the commotion.

There was a coach in front of them, immobile and helpless with at least two of its four horses dead in their harness and a bunch of Indians—six or eight of them, Donovan could see—on horseback shooting at whoever was inside.

"Jesus help us," someone muttered, and the patrol swept closer with a thunder of hooves and jangle of gear.

Chapter Thirty-five

All that mounted drill—hours and days and weeks of it—it all was forgotten in the headlong rush at the savages.

Even the lieutenant, riding out in front with his saber wildly slashing through the air, forgot about formation and command and control and whatever else a charge in mounted formation was supposed to involve. The lieutenant whooped and hollered right along with the rest of them.

Lieutenant Harmon didn't even remember to give the orders about taking up the carbines and preparing to fire and all of that, but it didn't matter, because as soon as the Indians were sighted not a half-mile distant and the horses started to run, everyone grabbed his carbine out and levered a cartridge into the chamber without having to be told.

Old Handsome acted like he knew what he was doing and was no slouch at trying to outrace the other horses. It occurred to Donovan to wonder what he should do if he fell off, but that sort of thinking didn't last very long, if only for the fact that soon there wasn't time for any more thinking.

Ahead of them the Indians figured out mighty quick that they were not alone out here with nothing but that coach to bother. But then, they would have had to be blind, deaf, and stupid not to know the patrol was onto them.

There was noise enough for the whole regiment, what with all the pounding and shouting and high-pitched yip-yip-yipping. Some of the more excitable boys started shooting when they were a good three hundred yards or more away from the handful of savages. It didn't accomplish anything more than to add to the general din, three hundred yards being way to hell and gone past the effective range of the Spencer's puny cartridge. And if that hadn't been enough noise to arouse the dead, Donovan had no doubt that the lieutenant would've had a bugle call leading the way if only he'd thought to bring the bugler along.

Oh, it was a heart-thumping thing, a cavalry charge.

And not something any sensible Indian seemed interested in standing still for.

The Indians put aside their hostility for whoever was in that coach and began scampering lickety-split toward the Arkansas River valley, which they said wasn't more than two, maybe three hundred miles to the south.

As soon as the Indians showed they weren't going to make a fight of it, the rest of the boys got the wind up—perhaps from knowing they were safe now from return fire, it being bad enough trying to shoot forward off the back of a running horse but nigh impossible to shoot backward off of one—and the whole bunch of yellow-leg soldiers began shooting.

Donovan did it too. He thought about dropping his reins, then reconsidered when it occurred to him that he could lose them and find himself on a runaway. He settled for tucking the tip end of his reins under his left thigh so he could use both hands on the Spencer.

He levered and cocked and fired and levered and cocked and fired. It was wild and exciting and kind of fun, actually. Exhilarating and then some.

His throat began to hurt, and it wasn't until then that he realized he was screaming as loudly and shrilly as the rest of them. He hadn't particularly intended to. It just sort of happened.

He could see bullets kicking up in the dirt in a loose pattern around and behind the Indians' racing ponies, but not many of them looked like they were putting the hostiles in any particular danger.

The situation didn't look apt to change, either, because the Indians' mounts, being lighter burdened than the heavy cavalry horses, began very quickly to increase the distance between them, their initial lead of three hundred yards or so soon lengthening.

Someone must have gotten lucky, though, or there was a very convenient prairie dog hole out there, because one of the Indian ponies folded its front legs and went down nose first into a slide.

The Indian who'd been riding it jumped off as light and easy as if the horse were standing still. He landed on his feet at a run, rifle still in hand, but quickly came to a stop when he realized—or Donovan supposed that he realized, anyway—that all of a sudden he was alone there with a couple dozen cavalrymen bearing down on him.

The Indian had been the last one in the bunch, and apparently the others didn't notice his horse go down. Not right off, they didn't, for they continued to ride just as hard and as fast as they could manage toward the southern horizon.

The Indian turned toward the rapidly disappearing backsides of his friends, but if he shouted anything to them Donovan couldn't hear it over all the noise the patrol was making.

The patrol was within a hundred and fifty yards by the time the Indian realized he wasn't getting help from anyone else and jumped for cover behind his fallen horse, which was now laboring to get to its feet despite a foreleg that was busted and sticking out at an angle.

The Indian took a moment to shoot the horse, then dropped behind it and started shooting at the troopers.

Donovan didn't know for sure who the savage was shooting at, but he couldn't hear any bullets coming close.

He couldn't hear the rest of the patrol very well, either, as old Handsome finally—with a perfectly rotten sense of timing—got his wish about running faster than any of the other horses.

Well, either Handsome accomplished the deed or everybody else had sense enough to slow down and let somebody else take the lead now that that Indian was shooting back at them.

Donovan and Handsome were even in front of the lieutenant now. Not that there was any disgrace in that, really. After all, Lieutenant Harmon was leading the charge with a saber in his hand, his revolver forgotten and still in its holster. And a long knife isn't much help against a repeating rifle.

Donovan decided the sensible thing here would be for him to slow a mite, too, and let the other boys catch up. By the time he recovered his reins and got Handsome's attention, though, he wasn't more than twenty or thirty yards away from the Indian lying behind his dead horse.

The Indian rose up, aimed dead at Donovan sitting there with nothing to hide behind, and pulled his trigger.

The hammer snapped on an empty chamber. Donovan was so close, he could hear the dull, metallic sound of it.

Damned Indian couldn't have had a single-shot rifle or even a Henry that carried a lot of cartridges in its tube but was awfully slow to reload. No, this SOB had one of the new brass-frame, side-loading Winchester rifles.

Donovan could see that.

The problem was that he could also see that this Indian was the same young guy who'd stopped by their fire just a few nights ago trying to beg some food and coffee.

There was no doubt about that. Donovan recognized the burn scar on the fellow's face and even the decorations on the little pouch he wore dangling against his chest.

It was too . . . too strange to *know* this man—boy, really—and sit here now and be shot at by him. Sort of know him, anyway.

It was just . . . it wasn't right, that's all. It just wasn't right.

Donovan had his carbine in his hands and a perfect opportunity to shoot, and yet he sat there and did nothing while the Indian reloaded. The Indian kid was nervous. Scared, probably. But then, he almost certainly figured he was about to die. He reached into the pouch at his waist and brought out a fistful of cartridges, dropped several of them, finally fumbled one into the rifle, and yanked at the lever to load it into the chamber ready to fire.

"Don't," Donovan called to him. "You can surrender. Give yourself up. Don't shoot."

He held his hand out, palm forward.

If the Indian saw the gesture, he ignored it. He aimed the rifle square at Donovan.

"Don't," Donovan said again, his voice weak and sorrowful.

A volley of gunfire ripped out on either side of him and the Indian jerked and twitched as two dozen guns fired and half a dozen bullets found flesh.

Bits of blood and skin flew, and the Indian boy crumpled on top of his dead pony.

Donovan didn't trust his legs to hold him and didn't so much as try to dismount. He just leaned forward over Handsome's off shoulder and puked until clear slime was all he had left to bring up.

Chapter Thirty-six

"You got a minute, John?" Ed Sims, carrying a cup of coffee, dropped into a cross-legged seat on the dry grass. The patrol was bivouacked for the night. Donovan had walked out away from the others and from the coach they were escorting back to Camp Horan—there were five survivors of the attack; the driver and one passenger had been killed—in an effort to find some privacy. He was feeling about as glum as he could ever remember being.

"I got nothing but minutes, Ed, and not a one of them worth much."

"You ever shot a man, John?" When no response was forthcoming, Sims said, "You don't hafta answer that. I know you haven't."

Donovan looked at him but still didn't say anything.

"During the war, John, I knew a lot of fellows. Nearly all of them was good soldiers. Good guys, too. You know what I mean?" Sims paused to wait for a word, a nod, something. When he failed to get it, he went on anyway. "What I want you should know, John, is that it isn't easy to kill. It isn't easy or natural or even right to send a bullet into another human person. But sometimes it's something that's got to be done.

"Some fellas just can't do it. Not ever. Not at all. I knew some during the war like that. I was friends with some of them. They went through the entire damn war and never once shot their rifles. Or else they'd shoot so they wouldn't be found out, but they wouldn't shoot at the enemy. They'd shoot way high into the air so they could be sure their ball wouldn't hit nobody.

"O' course, what those boys didn't think about was that the enemy, he didn't feel that same way. He was shooting back, and he was shooting to kill. Don't let anybody ever tell you, John, that those Johnny Rebs were cowards. They weren't. They were good men, most of them, and they fought hard. Whipping them never came easy.

"The thing I'm trying to tell you, though, John, is that the boys who couldn't bring themselves to shoot weren't just putting themselves in danger. That woulda been fair, if you see what I mean. Like if it was only them standing there and choosing to take the fire without returning it. In a way that woulda been okay. But it wasn't only them that the Johnny Rebs shot at. It was me, too. And all the rest of the boys in the outfit. And other fellows got shot and wounded and maybe died because those fellows on our side of it decided they didn't want to shoot their guns at another person. Do you see what I'm trying to tell you, John?"

"I see, Ed. God knows I see it. That's sort of what I'm trying to think through here."

"Right. That's good, John. I'm glad to hear that. Can I give you a piece of advice?"

Donovan smiled. "Ed, you walked over here with just that in mind, and I doubt I could keep you from giving it if I bashed you with a stick. If I could find a stick someplace, that is."

Sims returned the smile with a grin and the comment "Thinking is good, John. Thinking is exactly what you got to do so this won't happen the next time you're facing hostiles."

"D'you think there will be a next time, Ed? Back east the recruiting sergeant said the Indian fighting was most done. He said we'd just be guarding wagons and standing watch over reservations and like that."

"Hell, John, recruiting sergeants lie for a living. Everybody knows that. Do you really think the government would spend all the money it takes to keep an army in the field out here if it wasn't needed? There'll be a next time, all right. But next time you'll be ready for it. Leastways you will be if you do what I tell you here. And what that is, John, I want you to sit here by yourself for a while longer . . . I'll go on back in a minute and leave you alone to work this out . . . but, see, what you need to be doing is thinking it through and sorta preparing yourself.

"You got to think not about the overall stuff, see. You got to imagine all the little details. Most of all, you got to be able to *see* yourself pulling that trigger. And don't be bashful about the details. Think to yourself exactly what is gonna happen when you do pull that trigger. Think about every least bit of it. Think about the gun going off and that bullet coming out the end of the barrel.

"Think back to this afternoon. Remember how that Injun looked standing there with a repeating rifle in his hands and fixing to shoot you down. Try and remember exactly how that son of a bitch looked at the time. Then think about you pulling the trigger and a bullet coming out and hitting him in the belly. Think about the sound that bullet would make and how it would go inside that Injun's gut and how it would tear all through him. Think about the blood and him doubling over and dying from what you done to him.

"Think about every tiny wee least bit of it, John. And most important of all, once you've done thinking about all those details . . . what it would look like and sound like and feel like . . . then I want you to think about this being a *good* thing to happen. You know? I want you to think how this is what you're supposed to do. I want you to work out in your mind . . . right here tonight and not wait until the next time we're in a fight with Injuns . . . I want you to work out in your mind, John, that shooting the next son of a bitch Injun is right and proper so that when the time comes you'll be ready. So next time you'll pull that trigger and gut-shoot the SOB and not have to worry is the rest of the patrol standing there shooting at him for you."

"Kind of . . . visualize it happening, right?"

Sims grinned again. "I thought I just said that."

"Yeah, I guess you did at that."

Sims took a deep swallow of his coffee, which probably was growing cold by then in the thin-walled steel mess cup, and smacked his lips as if it tasted mighty fine, which their camp coffee most assuredly never did. "You want some?" he offered.

Donovan shook his head. Sims drank again, then stood. "You're first up walking night guard. I'll come fetch you when it's time."

Sims started back toward the cluster of waist-high shelters and scattering of fires that marked the bivouac, but Donovan stopped him. "Ed."

"Yeah?"

Donovan hesitated for a moment, then said, "Thanks. There . . . it won't happen again. I'll think it through. Like you said. If there's any doubt in my mind, any at all, I'll quit the outfit, Ed. I won't let you and the other boys down. I . . . I hadn't really thought about it like that, you see. It won't happen again."

"Hell, John, I never thought that it would," Sims said cheerily. "See you later, bub." He walked back to the campfires, leaving Donovan alone in the gloom of the gathering dusk.

Chapter Thirty-seven

Donovan belched, the taste of vinegar and onion pleasant in his mouth even this second time around. He puffed his cheeks out and held it in for a moment, then exhaled slowly as he looked around. The fringes of the parade ground were busy on both sides with idle soldiers taking their after-dinner ease, cavalry on this side and infantry opposite.

They had been back off patrol for, what—he had to think about it—three days now, and already he was bored with the routines of post. As much as he hated the inconveniences of patrol duty when he was out—and as especially uncomfortable as this last patrol had been in some ways—he had come to hate even worse the dullness of life at Horan. Stables. Fatigue detail. Drill both mounted and on foot. More fatigue. More stables. The pattern never ended and rarely varied. Even the food was boring. He belched again. It was better now that they had vinegar and a few other condiments to lend flavor to a deadly bland diet, but boring nonetheless.

He thought about walking over to the sutler's store for a sweet. But that greedy so-and-so Erickson charged a man ten cents for a two-cent bag of horehound candies, dang him. Donovan bought them sometimes. But he resented doing it every time, and tonight he was not in a mood to put up with that sort of aggravation.

What he ought to do with his free time this evening, of course, was go back to the barracks and polish his buttons and boots.

He was on the roster for guard mount tomorrow, and the sharpest, snazziest, best-turned-out soldier on guard received the reward of being named as the captain's runner for the twenty-four-hour guard detail.

Being the captain's runner was a plum, all the more so since the captain never required any errands to be performed. The captain was very rarely in evidence in any form, and his runner had a life of ease among the officers, with fresh coffee available all the time and trays of sweet breads laid out by the cooks. The officers had to pay for their luxuries, but the captain's runners and a few other select enlisted men posted to headquarters duties got to enjoy them.

Captain's runner was an honor given to the best-turned-out man alone, and in order to win it a fellow had to be sharp. Sometimes the competition was so keen they went as far as checking to make sure a man was wearing correct and clean issue underwear and socks.

Captain's runner was also a whole lot of work to achieve. Donovan had won it just once in the past, and he wasn't sure he wanted to go to all that much work again this evening.

And if he didn't win it, well, it wasn't so awfully bad walking guard four hours on and four hours off for the next twenty-four. In a way, it was a welcome break from the dullness of the daily routine.

He smiled a little, thinking about what the corporal always said when one of them bitched about guard duty: *You can catch up on your sleep next winter.* Of course, Donovan had already learned better than to believe anything like that. But it sounded kinda good.

He stifled a yawn and thought again about going inside and putting his gear in order for tomorrow's inspection.

Thought about it. Rejected it. The sun wasn't going down until late at this time of year, and the evenings out here in huge, empty Kansas were about as pleasant and nice as evenings can get.

The heck with guard mount. He'd give his stuff a lick and a wipe after call to quarters was blown. It would be good enough.

In the meantime, he intended to enjoy some peace and quiet away from the rest of the fellows.

He glanced around to make sure no one was paying any attention—he didn't want company or for anyone to think he was trying to sneak off and go "over the hill"— then ambled off toward the creek and the rare pleasure of the woodlot that lined its banks.

These rolling plains weren't anything like the soft and silent woods he'd known back home, but as dissimilar as it really was, this thin strand of waterside trees was the closest thing he could find out here to the places he remembered from his childhood.

Chapter Thirty-eight

He hesitated, not sure if he should announce himself or silently withdraw. That same woman, Sarah, was sitting on the log Donovan liked here along the creek bank, obviously enjoying the peaceful quiet here as much as he sometimes did.

Probably the proper thing to do would be to slip away and find another spot downstream where he could sit for a while. She hadn't come here to socialize, so that would be . . .

"Hello."

He felt a burning return to his ears and cheeks. While he'd been standing there trying to decide what to do, she had looked around and of course saw him as plain as plain could be.

He coughed into his fist and said, "I wasn't. . . . I mean, I didn't . . ."

"Is something wrong?" She sounded friendly and nice

and not at all as if she resented his intrusion. "Here." She pulled the material of her dress closer to her side and pointed. "Sit with me. Or would you rather I leave?" She smiled. "It is your perch, after all. You showed it to me."

"Oh, I . . . it isn't really mine, ma'am. Miss. It belongs. . . ." He sounded addle—brained even to himself, so he must surely be presenting himself as daft to this stranger. "You didn't mean that literally," he lamely finished.

"No, I didn't." She smiled again. "Come and sit. If you want me to leave, I shall."

"No, ma'am." He joined her, walking wide around her to gain the creek side of the fallen log. If he was going to sit there, though, he had no choice but to come quite near, because although the old tree trunk was thick enough and strong enough for all of its dozen or so feet of length, there was only a limited area that lay parallel to the ground and would provide comfortable seating. And Sarah hadn't chosen to sit near the end of the flat part. Nor did she shift away to give him more room. He was very conscious of her nearness when he perched uncomfortably close to her side. After all, it wasn't seemly for a soldier to intrude himself too near a married woman.

His forehead wrinkled in concentration as the implications of that thought came to him. "Ma'am?"

"Yes, Trooper? I, uh, I hope you don't mind. I believe you gave me your name the first time we met here. But . . . forgive me . . . I've forgotten it."

He snatched his hat off and held it in his lap. "Donovan, ma'am. John Donovan."

"Of course. Please excuse my bad manners. You were about to ask me something?"

"Yes, ma'am, I . . ."

"Sarah," she corrected. "Please call me Sarah."

"Yes, ma'am. I mean . . . Sarah." He tried a smile but was sure it was weak. "I was just . . . there's no wagon train in right now. I'm sure I'd've seen or anyways heard if there was one. And . . . are you an officer's wife, ma'am? If you don't mind me asking, that is." He knew she wasn't. There would have been plenty of talk if any of the officers' families had arrived, if only because there weren't supposed to be any families at the temporary little posts like Horan. The army said the officers could have their families with them back at Fort Riley. But not out here. They weren't even building officers' quarters to accommodate any such.

She was still smiling, so he supposed he hadn't gone and offended her with his nosiness. "I work for Mr. Erickson," she explained.

"I see."

She relieved him of the responsibility of having to think of something to say after that. "And I know what you do, of course." She laughed. So did he. "Have you been in the army long?"

Donovan shook his head. "No, ma'am." She gave him an exaggerated sigh, and he quickly amended that to "Sarah. Sorry, I . . . habit, you know."

"Yes, I do know, and it is very nice of you, John. Now. You were going to tell me about your army life."

He shrugged and said, "There's not much to tell. I've only been out here for a few months now."

"And before that?"

"Oh, I just joined up and came out here right away. There's nothing before that. I wasn't in the war or anything."

"There wasn't *anything* before you joined the army?"

147

There was a note of tease in her voice, and the question was accompanied by a smile.

Donovan's expression became serious, though. "No. There wasn't anything before I joined up."

"Oh, John. I'm sorry." She reached over and touched his wrist in apology. "I should know better than to ask someone a thing like that. In fact, John, I *do* know better and just wasn't thinking. I hope you will forgive me." She smiled again. "Goodness gracious, I find myself asking that of you over and over, don't I? First I forgot your name and now I've intruded on your privacy. You must have a dreadful opinion of me."

She touched his wrist again, and this time she allowed her hand to stay there. He was acutely conscious of the warmth that came through the light contact of her fingertips on his skin.

"No, ma'am. I mean Sarah. I surely don't. And after all, you were sitting here first. I'm the one who's guilty of intruding."

"Not at all, John. I'm glad for the company." She looked out toward the creek and the glimpses of prairie that could be seen through a thin veil of foliage on the far west side of it. "I'm glad for the beauty and the quiet here, too. Now that I know about this place, I've come to regard it as a refuge from . . . from everything. Do you feel that way too, John? Is that why you come here?"

"It is," he admitted. "It's quiet and nice. A man . . . a person, I mean . . . can think in a spot like this." He didn't mention that the thing he'd come here to think about this evening was the question of how it would—or should— feel to kill a man. That was something he had yet to resolve.

What he hoped for deep within himself was that he

would never again be tested; that his squad would not again have to shoot or be shot at. Empty plains, boring patrols, and escort duty beside wagon trains filled with pretty girls, that would be a fine way to serve out the remainder of a five-year enlistment.

"May I make a pact with you, John?"

The question took him somewhat aback. But he quickly recovered what little composure he had and nodded agreement. "I would be honored." This time there was only a very slight hesitation before he was able to manage the familiarity and add, "Sarah."

She smiled. "Good. Then I shall pledge to faithfully refrain from ever asking you what it is that you come here to ponder. And you, of course, must make the same promise to me. Will you do that, John?"

"Of course I will, Sarah."

"Capital," she said briskly. She lifted her hand from his wrist and extended it for a shake to seal their bargain.

Donovan grinned rather sheepishly when he accepted the handshake. And wished afterward that she would return her fingers to his wrist, but she didn't.

"I haven't seen you lately to congratulate you on your celebrity," Sarah said. He had no idea what she meant, and that must have shown in his expression. "On your victory in the footrace," she added. "You were very much the talk of the post afterward, you know."

"I didn't know."

"Oh, yes." She laughed. "There weren't very many who bet on you to win. I think every man in the infantry put their money on that tall young man of theirs. There was so much on him that your friends in the cavalry demanded odds to go against him. Did you know that?"

He shook his head.

"Can you keep a secret?"

"Of course."

"Well, I can't. So I shall tell you. Your corporal, Emil. He won thirty dollars betting on you."

"I'll be d—uh, darned." He hadn't thought Rathburn would have bet on him to win. Hadn't known the corporal's name was Emil, either, for that matter.

"Yes, you were quite the hero for the next several days after, believe me."

Donovan liked the way she smiled: She looked younger when she did that. And she had nice eyes. Sarah was far from the prettiest woman he'd ever seen, But he kind of liked her.

Liked, too, being told that he'd been the talk of the post and that the boys had backed him with their money. He hadn't known that. Nobody had spoken of it. Rathburn in particular hadn't shown any pleasure afterward.

But it was nice to know now. Very nice.

And so was Sarah very nice, he decided.

"Tell me," he said, wanting to keep this conversation going, "what is it you do for Mr. Erickson?" He'd been to the sutler's new store on several different occasions and hadn't seen Sarah there. He would have noticed, and so, for that matter, would all the rest of the boys.

Sarah's expression turned to stone. As if he'd just asked something that was deeply personal or even insulting.

"I thought we had a pact, John." The tone of her voice was accusing.

"I didn't . . . I was just trying to make . . . you know . . ."

Sarah gathered her skirts and stood. She didn't look quite as stern as she had a few moments earlier. But she did not look relaxed or happy now, either. "I have to go back now, John. Good evening."

He jumped to his feet, but too late for Sarah to notice. She'd already turned and begun walking back toward the noise and bustle of the post.

Donovan thought about escorting her back. That would be the proper thing to do. Except he did not think it appropriate now.

Dammit, he should have bitten his tongue rather than blurt out such a stupid question.

Not that he knew what was stupid about it, exactly. It hadn't sounded so nosy to him when he asked it. Hell, his whole idea had been to engage in talk that was harmless and inconsequential. Dammit! He hadn't known.

Well he knew now. And then some.

No, she wouldn't welcome his escort. Not now.

Maybe . . . He wondered if Sarah would even want to talk to him the next time. If ever there was a next time.

He grunted and sat rather heavily back down onto the log. Good evening, she'd said.

It had been good.

Now it was considerably less so.

He sat for a while listening to the sounds of water flowing over rocks in the stream, sat until it was near dark. Then he got up and made his way through the woodlot and out onto the grass again, back toward post where now the yellow glow of lamplight showed at the windows.

And he still wasn't really sure what he would do the next time he was expected to put a ball into another human's body. He'd imagined it over and over and over again. But he still didn't know and would not until— please God it never happened—until he actually had to pull a trigger with the intention to kill.

Chapter Thirty-nine

He didn't know why he kept thinking about her. It wasn't like she was pretty or anything. She wasn't. If anything, she was kind of dried out and wrinkled. And she was probably—he was just guessing, of course—probably ten years older than he.

Besides, she was probably married, too. To that greedy old high-profit sutler Erickson.

Of course, she'd said she worked for him. Would she have mentioned it if she was married to him? Perhaps . . . he didn't know . . . perhaps it was something she wouldn't have wanted to talk about. Like someone might think she was being disloyal to her man for walking out alone in the evenings the way she obviously liked to do. Would that keep her from saying it if she were indeed married to him? People could be gossipy anywhere, and especially so on a small and isolated post like Camp Horan where there wasn't much of anything that ever happened. Gossip, about things that were so and a fair number of things that weren't, was one of the principal diversions for the fellows.

Come to think of it, had Sarah actually said she "worked" for E. A. Erickson? Or had she said she was "with" him? Worked, well, that more than likely meant that she was employed by him. But if she'd said she was "with" him, that could mean a fair number of other things, too.

Not all of which he liked to think about.

Not that any of it was his business to neb into. No sir, not a bit of it. Whatever Sarah did, that was entirely her affair. Not his to consider, and whatever it was, she was sure entitled to it.

But he did kind of wish he could remember just exactly what word she had used when she mentioned Erickson.

He sighed. "Work" or "with"—mighty big difference between those two. It was just that he couldn't recall right now, not for positive certain sure, which she'd said.

That was, hmm, four days ago, and the exact sounds of her talking wouldn't quite come back into his mind, though he tried and tried now to remember and to get it right.

If she'd said . . .

"What're you thinking about, John?" Sims asked in a low voice from Donovan's right. They were outbound on what was supposed to be a six-day patrol, riding as usual in the loose column of twos, just the one squad of them with Rathburn in charge.

"Nothing."

"You look like you're deep in thought."

"Nah. Man's gotta have something to think with before

that happens." Donovan grinned. Self-deprecation was an acceptable, even a highly approved form of humor in the troop. Poking fun at someone else, of course, was likely to lead to fistfights and continuing rancor.

"If you don't wanta tell me . . ."

"Nothing to tell, Ed. Really."

From the head of the tiny column Rathburn's voice called, "At the trot now. Ho."

The corporal bumped his horse into a slow trot, and the others quickly followed his example.

Sims chuckled. "Five minutes. Not a second longer. Want to make a bet on it?"

Donovan grunted. "Not me."

It was no secret that Corporal Rathburn hated having to ride at the trot. Probably because he did not sit it well. For some reason, despite his rank and experience, he made a mess of the trot, bumping his backside on the saddle and undoubtedly annoying his mount every bit as much as the gait annoyed the corporal.

As a consequence, whenever the column was under Rathburn's control they moved at the trot as little as possible. The required march order of ten minutes at the trot was always cut short, often to as little as five minutes, and sometimes the gait was maintained even less.

By way of compensation for this departure from the normal order of things—and also because the corporal seemed to like marching on foot even less than he liked riding at the trot—they ignored the hourly ten minutes of dismounting and leading the mounts that was supposed to follow the trot.

Rathburn claimed the reduced time at a trot rendered the dismounted progress unnecessary. His custom—if only when well out of sight of the officers and other N

Troop noncoms—was to advance at the mounted walk for fifty-five minutes, trot for a scant five, and then drop back to the walk again. They dismounted and loosened the cinches only for coffee and meal breaks, and overnight bivouacs were apt to be established while considerable daylight remained.

The men, not surprisingly, rather liked conducting patrols under Corporal Rathburn.

Chapter Forty

Rathburn held a hand upright and drew rein, the column coming to a ragged halt behind him.

"Quiet," the corporal ordered. The command wasn't really necessary. They'd all heard it the first time.

The sound was soon repeated. It was a dull and hollow pop. The sound of gunfire. No doubt about it.

Rathburn turned to Randall Benson, who was next in line behind him. "Where do you think?"

Randy pointed. The noises, and now a third shot too, came from off to their right, toward the north beyond one of the countless low hills that made up this huge expanse of grass interspersed with brush-choked watercourses.

"Follow me." Rathburn's voice was crisp. He led out at a walk, increased it soon to a trot, and then almost immediately went into a canter.

The squad, for a change, stayed in tight formation

instead of straggling along the better part of a hundred yards.

But then, there were only thirteen of them, counting Rathburn. Donovan preferred to think of there being an even dozen in the squad and Rathburn in a separate category. Donovan didn't like the number thirteen.

The patrol clanked and rattled forward for a quarter mile, then slowed as they neared the top of the rise. Donovan didn't know if that was intended to save the horses' strength on the uphill pull or if it was to give Rathburn more time to see what lay in front of them.

With luck it wouldn't be anything more serious than a bunch of wandering emigrants shooting prairie hens. With an awful *lot* of luck, that is. The wagon road should be a good fifteen, twenty miles to the north if Donovan had it figured out correctly. There wasn't a great deal of likelihood that a train of movers would have gotten this far off the road.

"Indians."

Donovan wasn't sure who saw it and said it to begin with, but the word passed quickly down the line. Ed turned in his saddle and in a hushed and solemn tone passed it along to Louie Gordon and Trooper John Smith, who were riding behind him and Donovan.

"Halt."

They did. Qui   .

"In line now, boys. Form on me."

Jesus. There were only the thirteen of them. Twelve.

Still, the hours and days and weeks of unquestioning drill made it possible for each of them to wheel out of the column and into line with the corporal in the center and half a horse length in front of the rest.

"Ready your carbines."

Donovan felt the same fluttering emptiness in his belly as he pulled the Spencer from its socket and jacked the lever down and back up again to chamber a cartridge. He rested the buttplate on his thigh but didn't draw the hammer back yet. He didn't want to risk an accidental discharge that would tip the Indians to their presence.

"At a walk," Rathburn said, and they started the last few feet up the hill.

They hadn't gone more than a couple steps before Donovan could see over the grass-fuzzed crest. There were Indians down there, all right. Six, eight, maybe a dozen of them.

It wasn't some wagon train or isolated homestead they were shooting at, though. It was a small herd of buffalo.

Or, more accurately, there *had* been a herd there. The buffalo were on the run now, a band of perhaps a hundred of them disappearing toward the west under a yellow cloud of dust.

Immediately below the patrol, the Indians were dismounted in the midst of their kill from that herd. Four . . . no, five . . . dead or dying buffs lay in the grass. The Indians had no idea they weren't alone out here. They were off their horses and gathered together in a bunch, talking to each other and gesturing, no doubt recounting their prowess and accuracy in bringing the buffalo down.

It wasn't a war party, thank goodness, Donovan realized. Just a bunch of wild Indians collecting meat for the pot.

"At the trot now."

The uneasiness in Donovan's belly disappeared.

"At the gallop."

"Oh, Jesus!" Donovan blurted, and the fluttering fear returned stronger than ever.

"Charge!"

Chapter Forty-one

As soon as the patrol's horses broke into a run, the Indians heard them and scrambled onto their ponies.

One of the hostiles pointed his rifle in the general direction of the patrol and fired. He hadn't taken time to aim, and wherever the ball went it wasn't anywhere close enough for Donovan to hear its passage.

Still, they'd been fired upon, and if Rathburn was wanting an excuse for a scrap that was plenty enough to satisfy. The smoke hadn't had time to drift away from the muzzle of that Indian's rifle before Rathburn's carbine barked to return the compliment.

"Jesus," Donovan whispered again as he stuffed the end of his reins under his left leg, cocked his Spencer, and tried to aim into the bunch of Indians. Between the choppy gait of old Handsome over uneven terrain and Donovan's own nervousness, he knew there was no sense even trying to draw a bead on anything or anyone.

But he did pull the trigger. He did, by damn, pull the trigger. This time.

The Spencer cracked and lightly bumped his shoulder, and he immediately jacked another cartridge into place, cocked, and fired.

The other boys were shooting, too, and Rathburn was shouting and the Indians were running, and for a few seconds there it was heart-pumping, blood-heating, damn-all exciting.

That was the truth of it, and it surprised Donovan. But it was so. Charging down on a sworn foe and shooting at the sons of bitches ... it was exciting, and no doubt about it.

It didn't last long. Seconds. Half a minute at the most, Donovan decided afterward. Just that long, but it was enough to get him to breathing as hard as he'd done when he completed that footrace back at the post. He could feel the pounding of his own heart and hear the sing of stirred-up blood loud in his ears.

"Cease fire." Rathburn called. A couple shots rang out after that anyway. The corporal chose to ignore the infraction.

"At the trot. Now at the walk, boys."

The Indians—there were seven of them, Donovan could count now—disappeared over the next hill.

As far as Donovan could tell, there wasn't a soul on either side that had been hit in all that.

But Jesus, it was exhilarating.

Rathburn stopped beside one of the dead buffalo. The Indians hadn't had time to skin or butcher the cow, but one of them had already taken its tongue. Not much to share among seven warriors, but it was all they came away with.

Damned savages shouldn't have fired, Donovan thought.

Of course, maybe they wouldn't have if Rathburn hadn't chosen to come at them at the charge.

Not that anyone would ever know now. What was done was done, as the old saying went.

"Dismount, boys. We'll take a break here." Rathburn stepped down off his own horse by way of example. He cocked his head and peered toward the sky in the west. He looked a little disappointed to see that it wasn't late enough in the day to call for a bivouac, even by his standards.

"You did good here, boys. Damned good." Rathburn grinned. "And we'll have us some fresh meat the rest of this patrol, thanks to old Lo."

"Corporal."

"What is it, Gordon?"

"It's my horse, Corp'ral. Caught a bullet in the knee, looks like."

Rathburn cursed, then tossed his reins to Randy Benson and went to inspect the off fore of Gordon's mount. He knelt, felt of the wound, and cursed again when he stood.

"Strip your gear, Gordon."

Louie looked awfully unhappy, but he did as he was ordered.

"Shoot it."

"Corp'ral. Please."

"Somebody's got to shoot it, Gordon. You want me to do it for you?"

"I . . . yes, dammit. I'd like for you to do it. He's been a good horse."

Rathburn looked annoyed, but he lifted his Spencer

161

from where it hung at the end of his shoulder strap, cocked the carbine, and shot Louie's horse behind the ear.

The gunshot seemed loud enough to bring a chill into the afternoon heat, and the brown horse folded its legs and went down in a heap. It shivered for a few seconds and was still.

The death of the horse put a damper on the excitement of the scrap. It had only been a dumb brute, of course. But Donovan felt its loss, and he was pretty sure the rest of the boys did, too, although no one said anything.

Rathburn gave them a dirty look and said, "Horse holders up. Take your meat by the fours. Holders, let the horses graze. And not around here, dammit. Take them upwind a ways so they won't be smelling all this blood. The rest of you get your meat. Smoke if you want. We'll be here a little while."

"What about me, Corp'ral?" Louie asked.

"You know the way back. And don't be losing your saddle and headstall. I'll be checking on that when we get back to post. Take you some meat so's you'll have rations along the way. You got a knife?"

"Yes, Corp'ral."

"Got matches or something to start your fire?"

"No, Corp'ral."

"Here," Rathburn said in a gruff voice. He dug into a pocket and produced a small magnifying glass. "Use this. And don't lose it. I carried that since before Chickamauga. I don't want to have to go buying a new one after all this time."

"Yes, Corp'ral. Thank you."

"Don't thank me. Just hang on to my damned glass. And Gordon. Don't be building no fires for the night. Make one fire a day, about midday, and do all your day's cooking then. Make it so it don't smoke, and keep it small. You hear what I'm telling you, Gordon?"

"I'll not lose your glass, Corp'ral. I hear what you're telling me."

"All right, then. What the hell are the rest of you staring at? If you don't have better things to do than that, we can all just mount up and get back to our scout."

The boys scattered, Louie included, and got busy cutting thick slabs of meat off the buffalo lying there fresh killed for the taking.

Buffalo hide, it turned out, was almighty tough to cut even with a good knife, and the woolly coat was running thick with ticks and fleas that were busy looking for new and better places to live.

Still, Donovan had heard pretty much all his life how exceptionally good buffalo hump meat was supposed to be, and this was too good a chance to miss out on. He figured to pack as big a hunk as he and Handsome could manage.

Poor Louie, though. Donovan was glad it was Louie's horse that had to be put down and not Handsome. But if the time ever came, well, he hoped Rathburn or Ed or some-damn-body would be willing to pull the trigger for him.

Chapter Forty-two

Howland's Station was the unofficial turnaround point for the patrols going in this direction along the Smoky Hill route. More than a simple horse changing station for the stage line—which it had started out to be—Howland's was nonetheless too small to be considered a village. It might have been considered a budding settlement save for the fact that there was only the one enterprise in place there, that being George Howland and his several variations from a basic theme.

In addition to the draft horses he kept for the stagecoach relays, Howland also had a store that catered to the particular needs of emigrants, offering up such necessities as axle grease that was blessedly free of sand and grit, harness oil, cooking oil, and lamp oil—there were those who claimed it was all the same oil, just sold in different containers for different prices, depending on its stated use—or luxury items like fresh meat, pies baked in a real oven, and hot, hot water to wash with. By the time they reached Howland's, the movers wouldn't have seen a clean towel for more than a month or tasted anything that they hadn't brought all the way from the States.

Donovan guessed that George Howland did a pretty fair trade out here in the middle of nothing.

And he knew for sure that Howland was a canny man who understood who it was that buttered his bread.

Emigrant trains were viewed at Howland's as money waiting to be collected. But cavalry patrols were welcomed as the very boys who would keep the whole she-bang—sod store, sod-walled corrals, sod smithy, sod equipment shed, sod smokehouse, sod storehouse . . . and one huge, gloriously comfortable, four-hole outhouse fabricated from lumber carried all the way out from the wharves of St. Louis—from being razed by the damned Indians.

There wasn't anything too good for the boys of N Troop as far as George Howland was concerned. Well, not so long as you were thinking in terms of items that were cheap and plentiful, that is. George knew who buttered the bread, but he wasn't going to give up any of his butter because of it.

What he did do, and what the boys always counted on when they reached Howland's, was to set out a spread of comestibles the like of which would otherwise be found only in fond memory. Passenger pigeon pie and dried apple pan dowdy was the customary fare, and after a couple experiences at Howland's Donovan could get his mouth to running saliva by the bucketful simply by approaching within twenty miles of the station.

It was no different this time. The patrol pulled in, and Corporal Rathburn greeted Howland and the leaders of a party of movers who were laying over at the station while they did some wheel and axle repairs. While the corporal was busy doing that, the boys of Four Squad set up their camp in the usual spot on the grass not too awfully far from the outhouse, and Lordy, wasn't it a pleasure to be able to sit there in indoor comfort for a change.

Trooper John Smith was odd man out now that Louie was afoot and making his way alone back to Camp Horan. Smith and Gordon generally joined their tent halves to form a shelter. The previous evening, Smith used his rubber tent half as a groundcloth and slept with nothing but stars for a roof. Tonight it looked like there might be a rainstorm brewing.

"Ask the corporal if you can bunk in with him," Donovan suggested. Rathburn always carried two tent halves and slept in a castle of his own when on patrol. One of the many perquisites of rank.

"And get on his blacklist? I don't think so," Smith said.

"Better than getting wet."

"Huh. That shows what you don't know, John. I've seen how Rathburn does a man who's on the shitlist. Fella in our four before you came did something Rathburn didn't like. Emerson, his name was. Good man, too. He didn't last two weeks after Rathburn got peeved with him. He skedaddled in the night. And there wasn't any doubt why he did it. Apart from the obvious, when he took off he stole Rathburn's favorite horse off the picket line. They sent a patrol after him . . . because of the horse, not the man . . . but they never found him. He's prob'ly in Colorado Territory now, getting rich off the gold discoveries out there."

"Rathburn was hard on him, you say?"

"And then some. With the corporal there's never any doubt if a man's on the shitlist. It's well named, you see, because the first thing he does is volunteer his man to clean out the latrines. I don't mean dig a new one, neither. I mean get down inside and clean out the old ones."

Donovan's nose wrinkled at the thought. "Listen, back to this thing about finding you a place to sleep . . ."

"Oh, don't worry about it, John. I'll be okay. If it starts to rain, I'll grab up my stuff and go sleep the rest of the night in one of the outbuildings." He grinned. "Just think, though . . . a whole night's sleep without interruption." Which was another reason why Howland's Station was so popular with all the patrols. Instead of having to stand guard over the horses all night, when they were at Howland's they were allowed to turn their mounts into the corrals that were surrounded with six-foot-tall sod walls. That was a joy also.

And for some reason the Indians had never attacked Howland's. There were some who whispered that George bought off the tribal leaders with whiskey and rifle cartridges, but Donovan didn't believe that, and neither did most of the men who had enjoyed the man's hospitality. Such ugly talk came mostly from the flatfoot infantry and others who rarely stirred themselves very far past the parade ground.

Donovan and Ed Sims finished setting up their waist-high tent, then joined Smith in walking over to the station buildings with their mess tins in hand.

Their faces fell, and so did those of the rest of the boys, though, when they saw what was waiting for them there.

Howland had food set out on the trestle tables like always, but this time it wasn't the succulent pigeon pie or the baked apple concoction they usually got. Beans and bacon, dammit. That's all that was on the table.

"Sorry, boys. My cook up and ran off to Leadville with a greasy-haired man from New York City."

"Dammit, Mr. Howland, your cook was a man."

"Yes, he was." Howland puffed wetly on the stem of a fancily carved pipe. "Partly."

"Oh." The trooper who'd made the comment, Henry Thompson from Randall Benson's four, got a little red in the neck and ears and shut his mouth before he put his foot any deeper into it.

"Tell you what I'll do to try and make up for it, fellows," Howland offered. "Before you ride out tomorrow, I'll lay on some hen eggs. So fresh they still got chicken shit on 'em. Two eggs apiece, how's that?"

The smiles quickly returned at the thought of fresh eggs. Actual, honest-to-Pete fresh chicken eggs out here normally sold at a dollar apiece. Back at Horan, even a hard-boiled pickled egg lay Lord only knew how long before it sold for thirty-five cents. And two eggs for each man? That sounded pretty good. Not as fine as apple pan dowdy, maybe, but pretty dang good anyhow.

Besides, it showed the man was trying. That ought to count for something.

"Thank you, Mr. Howland, sir."

"Always happy to make you boys comfortable." White smoke from the pipe wreathed his head as he exhaled. "Especially this trip out. Emil tells me you ran into a band of marauders yesterday. Couple dozen of them, was it? He said you men of Four Squad fought them valiantly."

It had been seven Indians, not several dozen of them, but Donovan didn't say anything and neither did any of the other fellows. And the Indians had been hunting, not marauding. And nobody but Louie Gordon's horse got shot.

But then, they wouldn't want to say or do anything to disrupt the serving up of fresh hen fruit come morning, would they?

"Help yourselves to such as we have, boys. And don't be shy. There's more where this came from."

Donovan smiled. Beans and bacon. Alternating with bacon and beans. Whoopee.

What the heck. He took a fresh grip on his mess tin and spoon and stepped up to the table.

Chapter Forty-three

Damn hat brim wouldn't stand up like it was supposed to. It was sodden and heavy and dropped in the back like a damn funnel, directing cold water straight inside the neck of his slicker and down his back. He might as well have thrown the slicker away, for all the good it was doing him. About the only place it might have had a chance to keep him dry was under his arms. And because the air couldn't get through the rubber coating on the slicker, he was hot and sweaty, making his armpits wet anyhow.

It had been raining now since shortly before day-break, and they'd been riding in it from the get-go. Half a day now and no end in sight. The sky was as dark and gray as an old bullet from one horizon clear to the other, north to south, east to west, any way a man cared to look.

Not that Donovan was doing much looking. He kept his head down and shoulders hunched, and about as far off as he was interested in seeing was the back end of Monroe Gibson's horse.

As usual, their four was riding at the tail end of the column. Well, their three until they got back to Horan and Louie was issued a replacement mount. Donovan and Sims and Smith were at the rear anyway. They didn't have to eat any dust today, of course. The cold rain and mud that replaced it was not a blessing.

"Are we gonna stop for a nooning?" somebody called out.

Rathburn ignored him. The corporal looked every bit as miserable as the rest of them were by now.

"I got to take a leak, Corporal." That was Benson's voice.

And now that he'd gone and mentioned it . . .

"I got to too," Donovan added, loudly enough that he was sure Rathburn heard.

"All right, dammit. But there's no point trying to make a fire in this. We'll let the horses blow for ten, fifteen minutes, then ride on. And if it makes you children feel any better, my command decision is that we should stay right here on the wagon road in order to protect any emigrants who may be mired in this mud."

Translated, this statement meant they would be cutting the patrol a day short and heading straight back to Camp Horan instead of completing the half-loop north of the road like they usually did.

The thought of getting out of this rain and into barracks was cheering enough to warm them for the day and a half more it would take them to reach Horan.

"Patrol, halt," Rathburn barked, making the decision official. By then they had already stopped, Rathburn included. "Dismount. Smoke if you like."

Huh! It would take a sulfur match to get a pipe lighted in this weather. They likely wouldn't see sunshine again for days to come. And flint and steel would be just about as useless as a burning glass, with the air so wet and heavy. The boys who were addicted to tobacco would be fuming, no doubt. But not smoking.

"Hold Handsome for me, would you, Ed?" Donovan asked, extending his reins to Sims.

"Where're you off to?"

Donovan inclined his head to the left, away from the road. The changed angle made that side of his hat brim collapse and sent a fresh trickle of icy water inside his slicker and onto his collarbone.

Sims laughed at him. "Jeez, John. There's nobody around to see you pee, not for twenty miles probably. And none of us cares to watch."

"Ah, hell, Ed. I just, well, wouldn't feel comfortable doing it in the middle of the damn road. Okay?"

Sims grinned, and took Handsome's reins.

There wasn't a tree in sight. The patrol hadn't passed anything taller than a grass stem since they rode out of Howland's Station that morning. But off to the side of the wheel ruts there was a group of flat, rain-darkened rocks. They didn't extend above the ground any higher than Donovan's shins, but they were the tallest things around apart from the men and the horses, so he walked over to them.

A few leftover wildflowers were clumped close to the base of the rocks, looking thoroughly miserable in this weather, and behind them there was something white glistening wetly in the rain.

Donovan yawned as he stepped over toward the rocks. He reached down and began unbuttoning his fly while he was still walking.

When he was several paces distant from the rocks, he stopped, his jaw gaping open in midyawn.

After a few shocked seconds, he turned and bawled, "Corporal Rathburn. Come quick!"

Chapter Forty-four

At least he didn't puke this time. He wasn't getting used to this sort of thing. God, he hoped he never did. But this time he didn't puke.

The white thing lying there in the rain was a body. A human body. It had been mangled and cut up to the point that he honestly couldn't tell right off if the body was that of a man or of a woman. And that even though the body was stripped completely naked.

Clothes, weapons, accoutrements . . . any and everything the man possessed when he was killed was gone now, carried away as booty.

Cold rain had washed every trace of blood away, leaving the gaping wounds even uglier and more unnatural somehow than usual. Not that there should ever even *be* anything usual about something this terrible, but Donovan supposed now that indeed there was.

Between the bloodlessness and the pallor of death the

corpse looked waxy and unreal. It put Donovan in mind of what a figure in a wax museum probably looked like.

Except this was not wax here and in no museum. This person, whoever and whatever, had been alive not so awfully long ago, for the birds and mice and such hadn't yet had time to get to it.

Rathburn came, and but a few seconds after him so did the rest of the squad save for the horse holders. Randy Benson threw up, and so did Henry Thompson.

"Jesus. Oh, Jesus God," somebody kept mumbling.

"Cavalryman," Rathburn announced after only a few moments of standing there peering down with his hands on his hips and a scowl on his face.

"How can you tell that, Corporal?"

Rathburn bent down and picked up a shiny brass cartridge casing. It was the stubby, slightly bottlenecked, and entirely familiar shape of their .56-56 Spencer cases.

"Could be a courier riding between Riley and Colorado Territory," Rathburn ventured.

"Anything to tell who he might've been?" Charlie Ellis asked.

All Rathburn or any of them could do was shake their heads. The trooper's face had been smashed in, so there was no telling what he might have looked like. He had brown hair. They could see that but not much more.

"He put up a hell of a fight, I'll say that for him," Rathburn said. "Look at all these empties. Looks like he fought till he ran out of ca'tridges."

"That isn't all he done, Corporal. Look here." Henry Thompson had stumbled off a few feet away to do his puking. Now he returned holding something that was so battered it was scarcely recognizable as a Spencer carbine.

The carbine had been battered, probably beaten against

the rocks behind which the dead man lay. The hammer was broken off, and both the underlever and trigger were missing. The wooden parts of the buttstock were broken completely away, and the steel cartridge tube was bent and twisted.

Donovan wasn't sure, but it looked to him like even the barrel had been bent out from the breech, and the Spencer barrel was one mighty stout and sturdy piece of steel.

"He must've wanted to make sure those red niggers couldn't take his gun and use it against somebody else," Sims said admiringly. Ed reached for what remained of the Spencer, then with a stricken yelp dropped it and began frantically wiping his hands on his slicker. "That's hair on the breech there. It's got to be the guy's hair."

"He really pissed those Injuns off, didn't he? He busted his gun, so they used it to pound on him maybe."

"This was one gutsy son of a bitch, though, knowing he was going out but doing something like that anyhow," Smith put in.

"He was brave. No doubt about it." Rathburn brought out his pipe and bent low to shelter the flare of a match from the continuing rain.

"Ah, shit!" he complained aloud, and stood upright without even trying to light the pipe. The match sputtered, forgotten in his hand, until a raindrop extinguished it.

"What's the matter now, Corporal?"

"I know who this poor bastard is, that's what." The corporal stepped around the legs of the corpse and bent down to fetch something off the ground at the base of one of the flat rocks.

He held it up, and Donovan, too, knew who the body was. Rathburn had found the deliberately shattered remains of the little magnifying piece the corporal had been carrying as a burning glass since the Battle of Chickamauga.

The glass Rathburn had given to Louie just the other day when he'd ordered the unhorsed trooper to walk back to the post.

Louie. The dead man was Louie Gordon. He'd come north to the road and was following it back to camp. Or had tried to, anyway.

"Dammit. Oh, dammit," Rathburn snarled. "The son of a bitch busted my glass too."

Donovan heard the words and knew the truth, and there was a roaring in his ears like the sound of a great wind springing up.

He heard Emil Rathburn call poor dead Louie a son of a bitch, and it was too much for Donovan to bear.

All traces of restraint were abandoned to the surge of fury that welled up inside him. He leaped forward, hands clawing for the squad corporal's throat. He did it without thinking, and because he did it without any hint of warning he was able to press home his charge without any of them, including Rathburn, realizing what he was up to until it was too late for anyone to stop him.

Donovan bore Rathburn down, sending the corporal reeling backward. The two of them tripped over Louie's mangled body, and they fell heavily into the mud.

Trooper John Donovan was industriously bent on pounding Corporal Emil Rathburn's head into the ground, resisting with an unnatural strength the efforts of the other men of the squad to pull him away, when he heard rather than felt a loud, dull, oddly hollow impact that filled his head and took away all other senses.

The blow was the last thing he remembered.

Chapter Forty-five

"Christ, you were lucky, John."

"Thirty days in the cell is lucky?"

"You better believe it is. They could've given you thirty years, John. If they really wanted to, they could've stood you up against a post and shot you. You assaulted a noncommissioned officer, John. In the field. Technically, that makes it in the face of the enemy, as far as the army is concerned. Oh, yeah, John. You're plenty lucky, all right."

"Funny, Ed. I don't much feel lucky."

Sims handed Donovan his supper. Meals these days consisted of a quart dipper of water and a half-pound chunk of coarse bread. It wasn't a diet a man was going to get fat on, and after nearly a month in confinement Donovan's already lean frame was skeletal. He wasn't sure what he'd weighed when they'd brought him in here. Probably something in the neighborhood of a hundred and thirty. Now he suspected it was closer to a hundred and ten and might have been less than that.

"You know what I heard, John?"

Donovan didn't answer, but Sims went on anyway. "Word is that Rathburn told the captain to go light on you. He said he could see how you might mistake his meaning that day."

Donovan looked up this time. He made a sour face and spat onto the dirt floor of his cell. "Mistake hell. I heard what I heard, and it was a lousy thing for him to say."

"Dammit, John, you heard wrong if you think that. Rathburn was marveling that a man could be as tough as Louie was, busting up his things like that so's the Injuns couldn't use them, knowing the whole time he was gonna die but gutsy to the end. What Rathburn meant was a compliment to Louie, not a complaint."

"That isn't the way I heard it at the time, Ed. It still isn't. I just wish I could've hurt him when I had the chance."

"You shouldn't ought to be like that, John. You were wrong. Now, let it go."

Donovan took a bite out of the bread. It was dry and tasted like sawdust. It always did. He filled his mouth with water so he could moisten the bread and get it down.

"How's Handsome, Ed? Who's taking care of him now?"

"They turned him out with the remount herd. I saw him just the other day. He's all right."

Donovan nodded his thanks and bit off another mouthful of bread, following it with a swallow of tepid water.

"I better go, John. I'll be in here with you if I don't get back out there soon."

"Rathburn on duty today?"

Sims shook his head. "No. Nesbitt."

"You try for captain's runner this tour?"

Ed shook his head again and grinned. "Nesbitt owed me a couple favors, so I knew I could get stockade duty. I wanted to see how you're coming. Is there anything you want me to tell anybody?"

There was one person Donovan wished he could send a message. But he daren't. "No. No, wait. Maybe there is. You can tell Rathburn what I think of him."

"I'm telling you, John, you ought to be grateful to him. If I was you, I'd look him up first thing when you get outa here and apologize. Do that and I'd bet the whole thing will be forgotten. He won't hold it against you. He isn't all that bad, really.

"Y'know, if you'd bother to remember, the corporal didn't have to try and make things easier for Louie when he was unhorsed. Rathburn gave him that burning glass so he wouldn't have to go without a fire and tried to advise him how to keep from attracting attention to himself. He did what he could. It was just Louie's lousy luck that those Injuns spotted him."

"You know what I've been wondering about while I been in here? I mean, I haven't been so awful busy that I didn't have time to do some serious thinking."

"What's that, John?"

"It's about Louie. I been wondering why he didn't shoot himself there at the end. Why he stood there and let them take him like that. You know what I think? I think he didn't realize he was out of ammunition until he'd fired that last shot and found there wasn't another to use on himself. I hope . . . if it ever happens to me, I mean . . ." He didn't finish the thought. He didn't have to.

After a moment, he went on. "You know what I

remember most? I hate it, 'cause I guess it's the way I'll always remember Louie. But what I remember so clear it still makes me sick to my stomach every time I call it back to mind is how he smelled."

"But he didn't . . . Oh. I see what you mean."

The patrol was a horse short, so both Donovan and Louie Gordon's body, wrapped inside one of Rathburn's tent halves, were brought back to Camp Horan tied over Handsome's back, Donovan draped over the saddle, and Louie lashed in place behind it. Apart from being god-awful painful every time they went to the trot, the position kept Donovan's nose in close proximity to Louie's rapidly decomposing body.

Sims shuddered.

"Ed."

"Yeah, John?"

"Thanks, man. You're a real pal."

"Think about what I said, will you?"

"I'll think about it," Donovan said. But he did not sound like he meant it.

Chapter Forty-six

They let him out on a Saturday. Late on a Saturday. Donovan figured the bastards could have let him out earlier if they'd wanted to, but it was past retreat before they finally unlocked the door and let him walk out into sunlight for the first time in a month.

He had a clear-cut choice. He could hurry off to take a bath right away or he could go to supper. He wanted—needed—both. A month on bread and water puts a crimp in a man's belly. A month without a change of clothes makes a man pretty ripe.

They say a person can't smell his own stink or his own sour breath? Not so. Donovan could smell both on himself and didn't at all like either one. But the bath he could get after supper. If he bathed first, he wouldn't get any supper. He headed for the mess hall.

"Jeez, guys. Clear the way. Don't nobody stand close," Charlie Ellis announced once Donovan was close enough for him to get a whiff.

"You been wrestling skunks during your time off, John?" someone else asked.

"I don't want t' be the one to give you bad news, Donovan, but you was in there so long there's mold growing on your face."

Donovan grinned and rubbed the thick beard that had grown out while he was in confinement. He hadn't had a choice about that, there not being anything in the way of razors or soap in the tiny building that was Camp Horan's stockade. For the first week or so he'd thought the infernal itching would drive him quite thoroughly mad. Once the itching stopped, however, and the beard softened it had become comfortable to the point that he sort of liked it. Of course, he still had no idea what it looked like, but if it wasn't too silly in appearance he thought he just might keep it.

Now, in response to the teasing, he ran his hand over it as if smoothing and styling and said, "Handy, is what it is, Albert. Gives me a place where I can keep my pets." He pretended to pluck out a flea or louse, placed the imaginary creature in the palm of his hand, stroked it a few times, and then tenderly returned the invisible animal into the depths of his beard.

"Hungry, John?"

"Just a little bit, Ed."

"You go ahead an' get to the head of the line, John."

"Oh, Lordy." As the scent of the army chow reached him, food that normally was thought drab and dreary in the extreme, it smelled so overpoweringly fine that his knees grew weak and his mouth filled with saliva. "Beans and bacon. Boys, I never thought I'd be so pleased to be having beans and bacon."

Donovan held his plate out for extra-heavy portions of each. He picked up a mug of coffee and turned to find

183

Rathburn in front of him, an empty mug in the corporal's hand. The noncoms ate before the common herd, and apparently Rathburn was ready for a refill of the coffee.

Both stopped. Both stood silently for a moment.

Donovan thought about what Ed Sims said before. He really did think about it. But . . .

The moment passed. Donovan dropped his eyes and stepped carefully around Rathburn, then carried his supper back to the table where his four—their three now that Louie was dead and buried—customarily ate.

Chapter Forty-seven

There was wrestling planned for Sunday afternoon, and some footraces. Donovan was not at all interested, and not only because he was a long way from getting his strength back. There was something else he'd been yearning to do during the month he was in the stockade.

He left the post early, skipping Sunday dinner after devouring a huge breakfast. He headed immediately for the creekside glade and the fallen log where he'd seen Sarah before.

It was no secret that he'd been in confinement. It would be no secret, either, that he was free now. He was, quite frankly, hoping she would return to the spot today.

But not too early.

A bath last night in a tub of water shared by a dozen others hadn't made him feel anywhere near clean enough. Now he carried with him a sliver of yellow naphtha soap and a comb, and spent the better part of a half hour crouched, shivering and miserable—but cleanly, *happily* shivering and miserable—in an ice-cold eddy a hundred yards or so downstream from the log.

Once he was done washing and felt genuinely clean again for this first time since he'd last ridden out on patrol, he combed his hair back. Then he combed his face, too.

That felt odd. But sort of nice. He'd finally gotten a look at himself in a mirror back in the barracks, and he rather liked the way the beard looked on his lean face. It was dark and full, and if he did say so himself, rather distinguished.

He wondered what Sarah would think of it.

And hoped very soon to find out.

He lazed about inside a thicket of low-growing willows until he was reasonably dry, then dressed and made his way back upstream to the spot that he'd come to think of as his own. And Sarah's.

She wasn't there.

Not that he supposed he had any right to expect her.

He still hadn't come to any conclusion as to whether she was married or simply worked for the sutler Erickson.

And there was nothing that said she should or even by happenstance would appear at the log on this Sunday afternoon.

Still, a man can always hope.

Donovan sat. He waited. He plucked at a bit of loose skin beside his left index finger until it tore and became raw and bled just a little. Darn thing stung like crazy.

Back on the post the boys must have finished Sunday dinner and started the games, because from time to time he could hear cheering loud enough to reach across the sun-baked grass to the creek and beyond.

Donovan sat. He waited.

Eventually . . . he had no idea how long he'd been

waiting . . . he found a shaft of sunlight dancing and dappling the ground close by the water. The grass illuminated by the light was lush and soft and smelled sweet. He stretched out in it, luxuriating in the feel and the scent. And in the pleasure of knowing he was free to get up and go somewhere else if he so decided.

He closed his eyes and gave his mind over to the slow and not entirely unpleasant emptiness that he'd learned during the past month to induce.

Chapter Forty-eight

"Are you all right, John? You look so . . . thin."

She was there. Sarah had come. She knelt beside him now, and it almost looked as if she had unspilled tears bright in the corners of her eyes. For him? It was a thought not to be pursued. But even so . . .

He sat up and rubbed at his eyes. "I must've fallen asleep." Amazing if he had. He'd slept so much the past month, he hadn't been sure he would be able to sleep again for the next month and a half. Yet he had. The shaft of sunlight must have long since left his grassy spot, and now the entire woodlot was filled with the shadows of impending dusk.

"I didn't want to disturb you," Sarah apologized.

"You didn't. I was . . ." He didn't want to admit to her that he'd come here in the hope he might see her. Not out loud, he didn't. "It's late," he said instead.

"I'm sorry, I . . . I saw you leave the post earlier. So early. I didn't really expect I would still find you here."

She shifted her eyes away from contact with his. "I . . . had to work this afternoon." Donovan wasn't sure in the dim and failing light, but he thought she blushed when she said that.

"I'm glad you came." He started to rise, and Sarah took him by the arm to help him onto his feet.

"Oh, John. You're all knobs and sticks. They must not have fed you anything at all while you were in there."

"You did know what happened, then?"

"Of course I knew." She gave him a wan smile. "There are no secrets on a post this small."

"No, I suppose not."

"Are you all right, John? Be honest with me, now. Did they hurt you?"

"No. I'm fine. Really I am. I'm not . . . I'm not the one that was hurt." He thought for a moment about Louie and tried, really tried, to make his thoughts nice ones. They were sad enough, that was true. And it was terrible that Louie was dead. But every time he thought about Louie now the smell of his corpse came back.

"You've missed supper, John. Can I get you something? Out of the store, I mean?"

He'd missed lunch too, but he didn't say anything about that. Being here, seeing Sarah, that was more important to him at the moment than another meal. He could eat come morning. He wouldn't see Sarah again until who knew when. He only shook his head in answer to her offer.

But oh, what a kind and generous offer it was. He was sure she didn't earn much working for Erickson. Probably less than a soldier's pay. He stumbled over his thanks, making a botch of it, he was sure.

"Can we sit on the log for a little while, John? Would you mind?"

He smiled, and for the first time in more than a month felt good. Really good. "Until tattoo, if you like?"

Sarah nodded and walked close beside him to the log. She sat close too, close enough that he was convinced he could feel the warmth from her body bridging the few inches that separated them.

"Would you like to talk about it, John?"

No, of course not.

That was what he meant to say. He really did.

But the words that came unbidden from his mouth were "Yes. Yes, I would, Sarah. Yes, I really would."

Sarah took his hand and held it tight in both of hers while a torrent of sorrow and frustration and anger poured out of him.

He was still talking, she still patiently listening, when the sharp, brassy tones of the bugle call to tattoo reached them across the grass.

Chapter Forty-nine

Donovan yawned and clamped his jaw tight against an impulse for his teeth to chatter. Hot as the days were, the mornings could be chilly. Not cold exactly, but certainly cool enough to notice. As this one was. It made a man appreciate coffee and a hot meal in his belly.

The coffee and meal he'd had, thank goodness. He'd been powerfully hungry after having only the one meal yesterday.

Breakfast was over now and the squad was already loosely gathered for the fatigue call soon to come. At the north end of the parade ground, the infantry company's bugler was warming the mouthpiece of his instrument in the palm of his hand while he waited for the post sergeant-major to prompt the call.

"Hear about Billings?" Ed Sims asked.

"The guy in One Squad? What about him?"

"He's skedaddled."

"No shit. Last night?"

Sims nodded. "Must've been. He answered roll call last night, but he wasn't to be found this morning."

"Think we'll be forming a patrol to run him down?"

Sims shrugged. "Maybe. Maybe not. He didn't take a horse with him when he went. Either he bought a horse off some civilian or he left on foot, so I expect it'll depend on how the captain looks at it."

"I heard the infantry had three guys go over the hill this weekend," John Smith put in.

"Three of them?"

Smith nodded. "One on Saturday and another two last night."

Sims mused, "What does the infantry do when they wanta chase down a deserter? Send a squad out to run at double time after him?"

"Nah," Donovan said. "They load up a pack mule and send it instead. You know why?" Everyone did, but he said it anyway. "Because the mule's smarter than a walks-a-heap soldier boy."

He got the expected laughter. At the far end of the parade ground they could see the sergeant-major say something to the blueleg bugler who licked his lips and raised the bugle to his mouth.

The boys tugged at their blouses and checked to make sure everything was properly buttoned and tucked.

As the staccato notes of fatigue call sounded over the post, the ranks grew straight as the men stiffened to attention and waited for assignment to the day's details.

There was no deserter patrol, Donovan noticed. Apparently Billings got lucky with his roll of the dice. The captain hadn't chosen to send a patrol after him. Now all Billings had to worry about was thirst, hunger, fatigue, heat . . . and, of course, hostile Indians. Being alone on the prairie trying to get away from the post would be every bit as bad as being alone and trying to get back to the safety of what passed so loosely for home out here. Like Louie Gordon. Donovan's thoughts flitted briefly to Louie and he shuddered, trying to put the unwelcome memories aside.

Lieutenant Harmon barked orders to Sergeant Pfeiffer, who was standing in for the first sergeant—he was probably sleeping off a drunken weekend—who relayed the assignments. One Squad to woodcutting. Two Squad hauling hay. Three Squad to the post garden. Four Squad sawing lumber for construction.

That was all right. Donovan didn't mind sawyering. Especially if he was allowed to cut from above. Being on top was harder on a man's back than dragging the saw down, but despite that he didn't much care for being on the lower end of the saw because of the way the sawdust rained down into the pit and got all inside a man's clothing.

Still and all, sawyering was easier work than woodcutting any way you wanted to look at it, and any of it was better than garden duty, as far as Donovan was concerned. Whacking the hard-baked ground with a hoe always gave him blisters that would sting for days afterward whenever sweat got into them.

"Donovan."

"Yes, Sergeant." He held his back rigid and his eyes straight ahead, barking out the response in an approved military manner.

"You will fall out for separate assignment, Trooper. Corporal Rathburn will give you the detail."

"Yes, Sergeant."

Pfeiffer brought the troop to attention, saluted Harmon, and got a salute in return. The sergeant executed a snappy about-face and barked, "Troop. Fall out for fatigue detail!"

The remainder of the squad drifted off in the direction of the sawyer pit, leaving Rathburn and Donovan behind.

There was a look on the corporal's face that Donovan did not much like. Grim and determined, he thought.

Chapter Fifty

Someday when he was old and gray—if he lived to be old and gray—he was *not* going to tell his grandchildren about today. If he had any grandchildren, which he didn't really expect either.

He really should have throttled the corporal when he had a chance.

Well, he hadn't. And now he had to pay for that glaring oversight.

Donovan changed into his white canvas stable fatigues—*white*; of all possible choices, the fatigue uniform just had to be white—and went to the stable to scrounge a bucket, some gum rubber boots, and a ladder. Someone was bound to be unhappy about the ladder. Likely the boots and bucket, too. But Donovan wasn't worried right now about what someone else was going to be unhappy about later on.

He assembled those and gave some thought to the chore. A large scoop shovel was generally considered the proper tool for this sort of thing, but Donovan did not agree with that assessment. Too shallow. Too prone to spillage.

No, what was needed here was . . . Ah! There. Hanging right on the wall. Next to Rathburn's saddle rack. It was the corporal's own grain scoop. Perfect. Donovan added the dipper-shaped, half-gallon scoop to the pile of implements already collected.

Just one more thing, but easily found: a rope. A stable, any stable, is practically a repository for ropes, cord, twine, and such. He found a suitable length of quarter-inch manila hemp and surveyed the collection.

There was nothing else he needed. Unfortunately. No more excuses to delay.

He gathered it all up and lugged everything to the enlisted men's latrine.

Clean it out, the corporal said.

Climb down in there and bring it all up and carry the vile, stinking, nasty stuff well outside the limits of the post before dumping it.

Right. Piece of cake.

Donovan knew exactly where he would *like* to dispose of it. Corporal Emil Rathburn's bunk came immediately to mind.

The thought gave him considerable satisfaction as he maneuvered the foot of the ladder down into the eight-foot-deep slit trench, tied one end of the rope off to a post and the other end to the bucket, which he lowered into the hole, donned the rubber boots over his stockinged feet, picked up the grain scoop, and—after a few deep breaths of blessedly clean air—began descending into the pits of Hell. Or at least into an earthly equivalent thereof.

With nothing but a layer of rubber covering them, the soles of his feet hurt as he descended the wooden rungs of the ladder, and the deeper he went the harder it was to breathe the noxious fumes.

He thought about opening his mouth to breathe so as to avoid having to smell the dank and acrid stench, then as quickly rejected the notion. There was no telling what might be floating about in the air, and he certainly did not want to swallow anything that might be there. That thought would have been enough to turn his stomach had it not already been turning so hard and fast that it was apt to become dizzy.

Donovan groaned softly to himself as he neared the bottom of the ladder and felt cool liquid envelop the thin rubber of the boots.

He took another step down. The coolness was above his ankles, reaching onto his calves now.

One more step, he thought. Just one. Carefully.

The chill climbed his shin.

With one very tentative toe he sought the bottom. There had to be a bottom down there. Didn't there?

Ah. There. Solid bottom. With some relief he brought the other foot down off the ladder.

And felt a new and awful sensation as the thick, cold, clammy liquid slurry spilled over the tops of the rubber boots, filling them and trapping Donovan's feet and lower legs inside with pounds and pounds and gallons and gallons—well, it *felt* like that much, anyway—of . . . stuff.

Donovan tipped his head back and squeezed his eyes tight shut for just a moment.

"Aaaarrgh!"

Chapter Fifty-one

He wasn't sure he would ever feel clean again. He'd bathed twice already, once when he was supposed to be on duty and the second time before evening mess, and he *still* didn't feel clean.

And he probably would have burned his stable fatigues except for two compelling reasons; one, that he could not afford to replace them, and the other, that it was not beyond reason that Rathburn would send him down into the sinks again. After all, the officers' latrine hadn't yet been emptied. And Donovan most assuredly did not want to have to burn two sets of fatigues.

He would have to keep these, he supposed.

But he would not, he absolutely would not leave them to reek and rot in a laundry sack underneath his bunk until this weekend or whenever else he might find time to do his washing. The uniform had to be cleaned. And right damned now, thank you.

"Ed."

"Be all right if I talk to you from over here, John?"

Donovan looked to see if his friend was joking or if Sims might actually be serious about it. Ed, fortunately, was grinning at him. And sitting on the edge of his own bunk in his usual spot.

"Those laundresses."

"What about them?" Sims asked.

"Do they really wash clothes too?"

Sims laughed. "Yes, John. They really wash clothes too. Not all the guys want to bother washing their own stuff like you do. The women aren't only whores. Heck, officially they aren't whores at all. The army allows them here with the understanding they'll wash clothes. If they wanta earn a little extra on the side, well, that ain't the army's concern."

"They charge much?"

"For which kind o' service?"

Donovan gave him a dirty look and did not bother to answer.

"Does it matter?" Sims returned. "I mean . . . you weren't thinking of changing your mind, I hope."

Donovan smiled, barely, and shrugged. "No, comes to that, I expect it doesn't matter."

"Well, I'm sure pleased to hear you say that, John."

"I think I'll walk over there after supper and see about getting these done. Just behind the sutler's store, right?"

"Jeez, John. You haven't been over there yet? Not for, uh, anything?"

Donovan shook his head.

Ed, bless him, was a good enough friend that he didn't offer any comment about that.

Chapter Fifty-two

The setting was crude. But then, so was the rest of Camp Horan. It wasn't like this was a wart on a princess's nose. More like a bump on a pig's snout.

The entire back wall of the sutler's store was covered with wood that was carefully cut, split, and stacked. Donovan suspected he knew where the wood came from, even though Erickson had no work crews of his own and even though operating a store, even an authorized one, was not an official military activity. He was pretty sure that some of those stove lengths looked familiar.

All that wood was necessary for the fire pits, over which were mounted three massive iron cauldrons where the dirty clothes were boiled, then rinsed. Even though the fires had been allowed to die down and the water to cool here at the end of the day, he could still smell the warmly humid and somehow rather comforting scents of naphtha and lye that had always meant Monday wash-days when he was a boy.

Past the cauldrons there was a long, low sod house that had five doorways, each haphazardly closed by a blanket suspended across the opening. That, he figured, would be where the laundresses lived and . . . engaged in their particular brand of part-time work.

He stopped and studied the area for a moment, faintly disquieted by the thought that something was missing. It took him a moment to work out what it was he expected to see and did not. Clotheslines. There were no clotheslines. There should have been.

Then a last-minute shaft of the fading daylight caught and highlighted a speck of white near the eaves—well, where there would have been eaves had the soddy been a regular house—and he walked around toward the side so he could see better.

The roof of the soddy was built so that it started high in the front and sloped almost to ground level in the rear. A set of wooden steps was provided at the back end of the long structure so access could be conveniently gained onto the roof where the day's washing was laid out to dry.

It wasn't the most ideal clothes-drying system he'd ever seen, but obviously it worked well enough. At least things wouldn't be stepped upon by horses or soldiers or dogs or whatever while on the roof. And if this odd arrangement worked, well, you can't much quarrel with success.

Donovan walked back around to the front of the laundresses' building and wondered how to draw their attention. He certainly did not want to barge into any of the . . . what should he call them? . . . compartments where the laundresses might be found. With the men off duty now, the, um, ladies might not be alone in their domiciles.

Nor did he want to shout out for them.

He settled for standing there, laundry bag in hand, loudly clearing his throat until finally, at the far end of the soddy, one of the blankets stirred.

An infantry corporal emerged, stopped to turn and say something to whoever was inside, and then went on his way with his blue kepi set at a jaunty angle.

Moments after that, the blanket was drawn aside again and a woman stepped out.

She looked at Donovan, a smile half formed on her lips.

The would-be smile died stillborn there.

Donovan gaped at the sight of Sarah with her hair in disarray and the neck of her dress hanging loose and partially unbuttoned.

"Oh, God, I . . ."

"Oh, God, I . . ."

Both started to speak at the same time, their blurted words identical as to startled tone and anguished content.

Donovan turned and ran blindly back to the barracks, his laundry needs forgotten now.

Chapter Fifty-three

It wasn't so bad. Really. After all, he had no right . . .
There wasn't even the wee tiniest hint of anything
between them that . . . He certainly hadn't thought
that . . . It wasn't like he should've *expected* anything . . .
It wasn't that . . .

Donovan hefted the river-slick rock in his hand and
bashed it onto the leg of his fatigue trousers as if he were
trying to break the rock. Maybe the canvas cloth, too.

Cold soapy water splashed in all directions, arcing out
into the creek in one direction and thoroughly soaking
Donovan's waist and lower legs in the opposite. He might
as well have waded right on out into the stream, for all
the good he was doing trying to stay dry. Not that another
bath would hurt anything.

And while he was out there, he thought sourly, he
might as well just stay there. Sink right down to the bottom and be done with it.

He smashed the rock down into wet cloth again. Even

harder this time. The exertion and the noise were satisfying. Or as close to being satisfying as anything was apt to come right now.

This had *not* been one of his better days. Everything considered.

First Rathburn and his damned sinks. Then . . .

He hit the fatigue pants again. And again.

He . . .

"John."

He didn't look around. Didn't have to. He recognized the voice well enough.

"John, will you please look at me? Talk to me?"

He picked up the rock, paused to make sure he had a good grip on it—he didn't want to look even more the fool by dropping the damned rock—and hit the dirty clothing with all the strength he could muster. Water sprayed.

"John. Please."

He set the rock aside, turned the wet cloth over, and bunched it into a new shape; then he pounded on it some more.

"Soap," Sarah said. "You need to add more soap now."

Donovan ignored the advice and continued to pound. But then, it wasn't filth he was trying to exorcise, but his own frustration. And, all right, disappointment. Not that he had any right to be disappointed. Dammit.

He hit the clothes some more.

"Here. Let me do that."

Sarah knelt beside him. She took the wad of wet and flattened clothes from him—but not the rock—and began kneading lye soap into them with her hands. If the soap stung and burned, as he knew it had to, she gave no sign of it.

"Men!" Sarah snorted. She scrubbed, twisted, wrung. Soaped. Scrubbed. Twisted. Rinsed.

"I thought you knew," she said after a few minutes.

Donovan said nothing. He considered standing up and leaving. But that would mean leaving his fatigues behind, and he didn't want to do that.

"It explains why you were decent to me, though, doesn't it?" she said in a casual tone while she shook out his trousers, examined them closely for a moment, and then turned them to begin the process of soaping, scrubbing, and cleaning them all over again.

"I should have understood. No one has ever been . . . nice to me . . . like that before. There isn't any reason why I should have thought you were different." She rinsed the trousers again. They looked clean now to Donovan. But apparently not clean enough for Sarah. She started in on them once more.

"I apologize for not making it clear to you right from the first."

He opened his mouth, but no words came out.

She was so close beside him that he could smell her. Not just the soap, but Sarah's own scent. He was sure of it. And it aroused him.

He hated that. Resented it. Was embarrassed by it, too.

He'd been attracted to her before. Now . . . knowing the truth . . . the physical yearnings were almost overpowering.

If he grabbed her. Right here and now. If he took her . . . what would she do? Can a whore cry rape? Or would it make it all right if he paid her afterward?

Goddammit!

Damned laundry was a wet and messy process. He was wet all over. Not just at his waist and legs. Now even his face was getting wet. His eyes were dripping with water. Damn stuff was running all down his cheeks.

He sobbed, the sound of it coming from deep, deep inside him and lurching awkwardly out of his mouth.

Sarah stopped what she was doing and turned to look at him. Then she, too, began to cry.

Chapter Fifty-four

"I thought you knew, John. I really did."

He didn't say anything, if only because he had no idea what he could say. Not about any of this.

They were sitting on the log. The log he'd come to think of as his and Sarah's. Two hours earlier, he'd thought, been quite certain about it, that he would never come to this spot again.

Now . . . He was here. He was too spent, both emotionally and physically, to go anywhere. So he sat. So he listened.

"I didn't . . . God knows, John, that little girls don't grow up hoping someday they can become whores."

The word sounded exceptionally dirty coming from Sarah's mouth, he thought. Dirty—and painful, too.

"When I was little I wanted the same things all girls do: pretty things; enough to eat; and a handsome prince to sweep me off my feet and carry me away—my prince would marry me and we would live happily ever after." She laughed, but it was an abrupt and bitter sound.

"Do you want to know something funny, John? I'll tell you something really funny. When I was little and thought things like that, I had no idea what married people do. The private things, I mean. I suppose I thought . . . I'm not sure I even remember what I thought then . . . that the prince and I would both live in a big, beautiful house, and we would have children. The children would just appear one day. We would wake up and there would be a baby in the nursery, and I would love it and take care of it, and there would be plenty of wonderful food for all of us to eat. We would have pretty things to wear and be clean and never, ever be hungry." She sighed.

"I was really stupid, wasn't I, John?"

There was no answer he could give. He was the one who'd been stupid, not Sarah.

"I still believed that sort of fairy tale. Then I grew up, oh, so awfully fast, John. Just one night. That was all it took to teach me how things really are. One night repeated dozens and dozens of times after. My mother was sick, and my father . . . my stepfather, really; my real daddy died a long time before . . . my father came and got me out of bed and took me to his room. Mama was right there in the bed too, so I thought it was all right. But it wasn't all right, John. It was ugly and it was awful, and it happened again and again, and after mama died he wanted me to be with him like that all the time. So I ran away.

"I was thirteen. And I was knocked up. I . . . did that offend you, John? I'm sorry. I suppose I should be more polite in the way I say things." She sounded more annoyed with him, though, than sorry.

She sounded—he had to think about it for a moment to decide—condescending.

"I was pregnant, John. I was fourteen when I had the baby. By then I knew how babies were made, you see. And I did love him. I still do. He's a wonderful little boy, John. He lives at a school back home in Michigan. He doesn't know what I do for a living, but he knows that I love him. I tell him that all the time in my letters. And I will do anything I have to, John, so I can send the money to take care of him. Anything.

"I love him, you see. And I won't let anyone or anything hurt him. Not ever in this whole damned world. He is ten years old now, and if I'm lucky I will be able to keep doing . . . what I'm doing . . . long enough to put him through high school. If my looks hold out long enough, that is, and I don't get beat so bad that I die from it."

Donovan looked at her for the first time since they'd sat down here. If her looks held out. She was a plain woman, but not . . . He felt something lurch inside him. The boy was ten, she said. And Sarah herself was fourteen when he was born. That was what she'd said, wasn't it?

Which meant that Sarah was twenty-four now.

And he'd thought her in her thirties.

Six to maybe eight more years for the child to finish his schooling? Eight more years of . . . all of this. Beatings, she'd mentioned. And the rest of it. He shuddered. He didn't think she could do it.

But she sounded so . . . calm. Matter-of-fact. Certain of her own purpose and intent.

"I did what I had to, John. Oh, I tried other things. Even when Bobby was born . . . did I tell you that his name is Bobby? Robert, actually. Robert Walter Wallace. Anyway, John, even after Bobby was born I tried to take care of him. I tried to work at honest and respectable things. But there isn't much that a woman can do and

209

even less that people will hire a girl for. And, of course, there was no hiding the fact that I was not a 'good' girl. I had Bobby. That was all the proof needed. So no matter where I went or what I tried to do, the gentlemen wanted to take me into the pantry or behind the woodpile.

"No matter that I said I didn't want to. If I wanted to keep the job, whatever the stupid job, that was always a part of it. And after all, virtue is something that can only be lost once. Believe me, that was explained to me many a time. Once the yolk is broke, you can't make the egg whole again.

"And it was . . . just too much. By the time Bobby was a year and a half, I knew there was only the one thing for me. So I started in to whoring. I wasn't very good at it. I'm not pretty and never have been. But that's something that 'most any woman can make her way by. There's always some fool randy enough and blind drunk enough that even an ugly woman can get by. So I went to whoring, and I made enough that I could put Bobby into that school. He started there when he was four and there he still is, and I love and miss him every day of my life.

"And if I could think of some way, John, *any* way, that I could manage for him and not have to do this, well, I'd do it. But there isn't any other way. None that I know of. And so I'll keep on doing this until Bobby finishes his school or else I'm dead, whichever of those happens the sooner."

"I wish . . ." They were the first words Donovan had spoken since they sat here, and they were anything but helpful.

"Yes," Sarah said. "So do I. But wishing doesn't do a damned thing, John. Believe me, because that is something I know about. There is no handsome prince, and there won't be any fine house filled with food and happiness, either. So wish me no wishes, John Donovan, for Sarah Wallace is doing what she has to. Do you understand that, John? Do you?"

He didn't. The reality was that he couldn't.

But he was trying.

Chapter Fifty-five

"Donovan!"

"Yes, Corporal."

"Front and center."

"Yes, Corporal." He hustled at the double-quick, holding himself stiffly erect against a sudden impulse to quail and run in the opposite direction. He faced more than just Rathburn this time. The troop sergeant-major was there, and behind him the lieutenant and behind him the captain, and nothing good could come from an assemblage of all of those.

The captain gave him a look like he was dog crap fouling the bottom of the captain's boot.

The lieutenant scowled and barked at the sergeant-major.

The sergeant-major spat and issued an order to the corporal.

And the corporal looked pleased to be able to deliver the message to Trooper Donovan.

"You were absent from roll call last night and absent from the barracks without leave at lights out," Rathburn accused.

"Yes, Corporal." He wondered, out of idle curiosity, what the bunch of them would do if he just denied that immutable truth. If he just stood there braced at attention and swore he'd been there. Oh, he bet they'd squawk and cuss on him then.

Probably make the punishment the worse, of course, but it would almost be fun to say it just to see their faces.

Rathburn would turn purple and bust something, more than likely. Yes sir, it was something to think about, all right.

"Three days on the wheel, Donovan. And if you continue this way, it will only get worse for you. Am I making myself clear to you, Trooper?"

"Yes, Corporal." The wheel. God! He'd rather have three months in the stockade than three days on the wheel.

Last night he should have . . . except no, dammit. He'd known the rules. He'd heard the bugle calls. And he'd continued to sit there with Sarah. Talking some. Listening plenty. Hadn't come up with any sort of idea that would make things different from what they were. But . . . he wasn't so shocked and hurt now as he'd been to start with when he first learned of . . . the way things were.

He didn't like it. God knew he didn't like it. But now he knew. For whatever that was worth.

"Report to me in the wagon park, Donovan. You have ten minutes if you want to get a drink or take a leak, whatever."

"Yes, Corporal. Thank you, Corporal."

In truth, Rathburn was being more generous than

Donovan might have expected. He didn't have to give him that chance to visit the latrine. Or, it also occurred to him, a chance to run if he wished.

Maybe that was it. Maybe Rathburn was trying to goad him into going over the hill now so they could chase him down and put him in prison for the next twenty damned years or so.

Well, they weren't going to get him that easy. He'd do his days on the wheel, and damn them every one.

"You're dismissed, Donovan."

"Yes, Corporal. Ten minutes." He executed the most perfect about-face he'd ever managed and marched stiffly off in the direction of the barracks. If he was going to be on the damned wheel, it wasn't going to be while he was in his best uniform, and that was for sure.

Chapter Fifty-six

Oh, God! He hadn't known anybody could hurt this bad. The log had been bad. They said the barrel was worse. With the barrel they made you stand barefoot on the top of an empty barrel. That was all. It didn't sound like much of a punishment. But the barrel was empty and there was no top on it. The soldier—victim was more like it—had to stand on the sharp edges of the rims. They said that in no time at all those edges cut into a man's feet and felt like they were knives. They said the barrel was Hell.

But now Donovan knew Hell for sure, and it was the wheel.

Damned wheel was another one that didn't sound so awfully bad when you heard about it.

They took a guy over to one of the big freight wagons, one with a wheel maybe five feet tall. And they tied him to it. Spread-eagle. That's all there was to the wheel. Didn't sound that terrible, really.

The thing was, your hands were extended out to the

sides. Straight out. Not raised so that a man could take his weight onto them if he wanted and not low to his sides so he could kind of push up against them and hold himself up that way, but straight out so he had practically no leverage or power to hold his weight. Any attempts to take his weight onto his arms or shoulders wouldn't last much more than seconds because of the awkward angle and the fact that a person's muscles just aren't built to do that.

So pretty much all of a man's weight was put onto his legs. And that, too, sounds innocent enough. Even comfortable. After all, folks spend about half their time walking or standing upright on their own hind legs. Certainly that was how Donovan saw it the first time he heard about the wheel.

But what was explained to him then—and so painfully demonstrated to him now—was that the spread-eagle position of a man on the wheel would not allow him to take his weight onto the bone structure of his legs.

With his feet held as wide apart as the width of the wagon wheel permitted and lashed in place there, his whole body weight was held up by the strands of long muscle on the insides of the thigh and groin.

And those muscles are not designed or intended to resist weight. Not for more than seconds at a time. Most definitely not for hour after hour.

And on the wheel that was what was required. A man was put onto the wheel soon after morning fatigue. He stayed there until retreat was blown. He stayed there for the post's entire working day. Heat of summer, cold of winter, wind or rain or snow, he stayed there. Couldn't change position; couldn't scratch an itch.

Those things were annoying. But the pain. The pain was excruciating. First the muscles along the insides of the thighs began to hurt. So the soldier tried to take his weight onto his arms. After half a minute or less he'd be forced to sag down onto his legs again, and the pain would return. But worse and steadily growing.

An ache would turn into a burn, the burn into fire, the knives and spears of fire into agony. And it did not end, would not end, until at the end of the day his buddies came to carry him back to barracks so he could lie writhing and twisting in misery on his bunk, the insides of his thighs still afire, the muscles involuntarily twitching and jumping like frog's legs in a hot skillet.

The first day Donovan thought he would die on the wheel.

The second day he wished he would.

By the end of the third day he scarcely knew if he was alive or dead when Ed Sims and John Smith half carried, half dragged him across the parade ground to the N Troop barracks.

Donovan was barely conscious. He had no strength left in him and was not sure he would ever recover the full use of his legs. The fire in them ran from hip to knee, and the pain did not stop now even when they took him off the wheel for the last time.

At the far end of the parade ground he could see Rathburn in deep conversation with the sergeant-major and Lieutenant Harmon, damn them all. Damn them all.

The pain was so bad that he was crying. The pain was so bad that he was not ashamed that he was crying.

Smith and Sims carried him to his bunk and laid him there with a blanket over him.

"I'll go find some more of that liniment," Sims offered.

"And don't worry about trying to make it to the mess hall," Smith said. "We'll bring something to you."

"You'll make it, guy."

"It's all over now," Smith told him. "All over."

Donovan hoped so. He couldn't take any more. The wheel, that damned wheel, used him up and spit out the gristle. All that was left of him now was a little bit of bone, and even that bit was burning.

He closed his eyes and concentrated on waiting out the pain.

Chapter Fifty-seven

The last time he'd drawn company punishment, after he carried the log, Rathburn detailed him to light duty afterward in what Ed Sims said was a sort of unspoken and unacknowledged custom.

Not this time.

Sick and weak and shaking as he was after being on the wheel for three days, Donovan was assigned to split and load wood.

Even riding upstream along Smith's Creek was painful, as the wagon bounced and jolted over every rut or rock along the way. Working once they got there was but a continuation of the agony he'd endured on the wheel.

The other boys tried as best they could to make things easier on him, but Rathburn was there, damn him, watching over the wood detail, watching Donovan in particular. Any attempt to dog the work brought a sharp warning from the corporal. And Donovan knew in his belly that

Rathburn would like nothing better than an excuse to send him back onto the wheel.

He spent the morning splitting sawed chunks into stove lengths, collapsed during the noon break, and then managed somehow to get through an afternoon of loading the newly split wood onto the wagon ready to carry it back to the post for stacking and drying.

He was miserable. He was also damned well determined that Rathburn would not get the better of him. Making it through the last couple hours of the detail on nothing but grit and raw nerve, he had to be helped off the wagon and into the barracks when they returned in time to change out of their stable fatigues and into blues for roll call and evening mess.

"Come on, John."

"I can't, Ed. Leave me be."

"You've got to eat, man. You can't keep your strength up if you don't eat something."

"You go ahead. Don't mind me."

Both Sims and Smith brought food back to him. He was lying on his bunk, chewing on a piece of cold pork, the insides of his thighs twitching and aching, when a man named Robinson found him.

Robinson was in One Squad, and Donovan doubted he'd passed a dozen words with the man since he'd joined N Troop.

"There's somebody wants to see you, Donovan."

"If it's Rathburn, tell him . . ." Donovan shook his head. "No, on second thought, you better not."

"It ain't your corporal, mister." Robinson gave him a rather strange look and added, "I don't know what you got that the rest of us don't, Donovan, but it's one of the laundresses as wants to talk to you."

"Me?"

"Yeah. Tall, skinny, kinda homely woman. I dunno her name, but she grabbed my shirtsleeve and asked would I bring a message to you. Something about . . . I'm not sure how she meant this, but something about a log?"

"He was on wood detail today," Smith said as he and the rest of the squad crowded close around Donovan's bunk. Apparently, mention of a laundress was more than enough to arouse the interest of everyone nearby. And the idea that one of them might wish to send a message to a particular soldier . . . that was nigh unheard of.

"He wouldn't have anything to do with where the wood goes," Charlie Ellis observed. And then with a cackle he added, "But I'd be glad to walk over there and discuss this situation with her."

"Look, dammit," Robinson said with a snort, "all I'm trying to do here is deliver a message. Is that all right with you? She said something about Donovan and a log. Said he'd know what she meant. Now, that's all I'm saying; that's all I know."

"Do you know what she would've meant by that, John?"

"I'm not sure that I do, Ed," he lied. He didn't want the rest of the squad to know what he was about. For sure he did not want any of them to follow him away from the post.

"Help me up, will you?"

They did, the rest of the squad helping to pull him to his feet. His balance was iffy and his stance uncertain, but he managed an upright posture, swaying slightly but braced and determined.

"Excuse me, fellas. I got to go take a leak."

"Sure you do," Ellis said with open skepticism. But none of the boys in Four Squad followed him when he slowly and with great caution teetered and wobbled his way out of the barracks and past the enlisted men's latrine on his way down to the creek.

Chapter Fifty-eight

She was waiting for him at the log. When Sarah saw him she rushed to meet him, and he leaned on her arm the last few steps. She helped ease him down onto the log and continued to cling to his hand even after she sat there close at his side.

"You don't look good, John. You don't look good at all."

He grinned. "If you think it's bad from your side of my eyeballs, you ought to try it from in here."

"Oh, John. I'm so sorry."

He shrugged. But he was pleased with her concern.

Sarah stroked his arm and clung to his hand, and despite the aches and pains that infested his every joint and muscle, he could feel the impact of her presence. He felt, well, *better* for having her near.

"There's something I was wanting to tell you, Sarah. Something I thought of while I was, uh, while I had so much time on my hands for thinking." He grinned again.

"While I didn't have much else to do, you see, and needed something to keep me occupied, like."

"That's nice, John, but . . ."

"No, let me tell you. Please."

"All right."

"I mean, it's none of my business, but . . ."

She waited for him to go on.

"I know where you can get a job. A real job, I mean."

"It costs an awful lot to keep my son in school, John. There's only the one job I know of that a woman can do to make that kind of money."

"Sure, but what I was thinking, see, is that you wouldn't need so awful much if . . . if your boy was there with you. Have you thought about that? If you could make a decent wage, even a little one, it should be all right if you could have him there with you. You could take care of him yourself. Teach him. Tend to him. And he'd be able to see that his mama was a decent woman. He'd be right there to see that."

"I don't . . . I hadn't thought about anything like that."

"Well, do think about it."

"What would the job be, John?"

"Cooking. You can cook, can't you?"

"I suppose so. Some."

"You wouldn't have to cook fancy. Just a lot. There's a stagecoach relay station west from here on the road. Howland's, it's called. George Howland, he's a good man. And he needs a cook. His ran off to the Colorado gold fields. He was complaining about it the last time our patrol was there."

"John, the last time you rode on a patrol was more than a month ago. You've been in the stockade ever since. You don't know if that job is still open or not."

"That's true, Sarah, but I thought about that too while I

was doing all this thinking." He smiled at her. "You aren't going to trip me up that easy. What I figured out, see, is that even if there isn't that job available, you could still find honest work. You could still send for your kid to come join you and live with you wherever you got a job. At Howland's, that would be good. But if he's already found a cook, why, you just keep on going. All the way to Colorado, if need be.

"Why, if there's gold fever you know there's jobs there wherever the men are. Respectable jobs, I mean. Cooking. Washing clothes. All that sort of thing. You could open your own café in one of the gold camps. Take in washing. Whatever. And your boy could be right there with you. It wouldn't take much for two people to get along."

"It's a nice thought, John, but . . ."

"Don't give me no 'but' for an answer. I've thought about this aplenty, let me tell you. If you really *want* to do it, well, you can. I know you can. If you was to really want to."

"It sounds . . . scary."

"But it would work, Sarah. It would work fine. And nobody need ever know you've ever done anything but cook for a living. Out here, Sarah, a man is whatever he says he is, and with whatever name he wants to claim. You could say you was a widow lady, and who would know different. No one, that's who. It would work, Sarah. I know it would."

"It sounds nice, doesn't it."

"Yes. It does."

"And you, John? Where would you be while I was raising my son?"

"I . . . I signed up for five years, Sarah. I don't have much choice until then."

"Oh, John." She grabbed tighter onto his arm and shook him just a little. "You can't stay here for five years. You can't. That's what I wanted to see you about tonight, John. I . . . I hear things, you know. We girls know more about the goings-on at this post than the officers do, let me tell you. And I know . . .

"John, they're going to break you. They're starting to get a lot of desertions, you know. Mostly from the infantry company. But the Seventh is losing men too, and your colonel . . . they say he's really angry about it and that he doesn't like to be crossed, not about anything. They say he wants an example made so the rest of the soldiers won't run off like some already have. And John . . . they say they've picked you to be that example. They intend to break you, John. They will keep after you until you snap and do something really awful or until you steal a horse and run off with it, and then they will put you on trial and either shoot you or send you off to prison for years and years."

"I've been a pretty good soldier, Sarah. I can be an even better one."

"That doesn't matter, John. This colonel . . . he's back at Fort Riley or someplace . . . he wants there to be one example made in each and every duty post. You are the trooper they've picked for Camp Horan, John. The captain told the sergeants to work out among themselves who they should go after, and the sergeants decided on you.

"If it makes you feel any better, John, Corporal Rathburn didn't want you to be the one. Rathburn said you had the makings of a good trooper in you. But the sergeant-major and the others wanted it to be you. The others picked you, I think, so it wouldn't have to be one of their own. Emil was voted down when he tried to keep you.

"If you . . . if you stay here, John, they will break you.

Maybe even kill you. You have to run away. Just don't steal a horse when you do it, and don't get caught."

"I don't think I could do that, Sarah. Not if . . . jeez, I can't believe I'm saying this, but . . . I wouldn't want to go over the hill if you're still here. I think . . ." He couldn't get the rest of the words out. Couldn't believe, either, that he actually had them in his head. She wasn't but a post laundress, after all, which as she herself said meant she wasn't but a cheap whore. And no sensible man would want anything to do with a woman like that. Especially when they'd never, well, *done* anything together.

He'd never so much as kissed her, for God's sake.

And it was stupid, really and truly stupid, for a man to get himself involved with a woman like that.

But then, he himself was the one telling her that she could quit being a woman like that. That she could start over and be and do whatever she wanted in this open, empty, brand-spanking-new country out here.

He . . .

The brassy notes of tattoo reached across the prairie, and Sarah abruptly stood. "We have to go back now, John. It wouldn't do for you to be late again."

"No, I reckon it wouldn't at that." He came to his feet, sharp pains stabbing through his thighs and upper legs. He stood hunched halfway over, like a man twice, three times his age.

"John, think about what I said."

"I will. If you'll think about what I told you, too."

"I . . . I'll think about it. I promise."

"Then so will I."

She leaned forward and gave him a dry, soft kiss on the cheek. Then she was gone, rushing back in the direction of the camp.

Donovan limped along much more slowly after her. No, it really would not do for him to be absent again, even if he didn't believe everything that Sarah told him about the captain and the noncoms.

Chapter Fifty-nine

"Donovan."

"Yes, Corporal?"

"Special duty assignment for you."

"Yes, Corporal."

"The cooks say the grease sump is getting full. Draw a spade from the quartermaster. I want you to dig a new sump. Sergeant McNown will tell you where. Then fill in the old one. You got that, Donovan?"

"Yes, Corporal."

"Donovan."

"Yes, Corporal?"

"I have something for you today that's just up your alley."

"Yes, Corporal."

"We need to inspect the back wall of the mess hall, and the stove wood is in the way. You're to move the wood ten feet away from the wall and restack it. But neat, now. Tidy."

"Yes, Corporal."

"Donovan."

"Yes, Corporal?"

"You didn't move the woodpile back where it belongs yesterday. You knew they were done with the inspection. You will move the wood back today."

"Yes, Corporal."

"And you'll see the lieutenant for company punishment after you're done. Maybe next time you'll remember to do what you're told, Trooper."

"Yes, Corporal."

"My God, John. Are you all right?"

"I'm fine, Ed. Just fine." He would have lifted his head to look at his friend, but he was too damned tired to do so.

At least he would have been able to raise his head. He doubted he could have raised his arms to defend himself if there were a dozen Cheyenne warriors coming at him.

"What was it today?"

"Moved the wood back against the mess hall wall. Restacked about half of it. Then I had to report to Lieutenant Harmon. He had me carry the log for an hour." He managed a smile. "Apart from that, though, I've hardly done a thing the whole day long."

"Jesus!" Sims blurted.

"Don't say that," Donovan said. "Next thing you'll get Him pissed off at me too." He smiled. But he half believed it.

"Donovan."

He opened his eyes with a groan. He'd spent the day

229

cleaning out the officers' latrine—which hadn't been half as hard as emptying the enlisted men's, and anyway he was almost getting used to it now—and he'd thought he was done for the day. But now they were coming for him after hours in the barracks too, it seemed.

He looked around but didn't see Rathburn or Pfeiffer or any of the other noncommissioned officers.

"Donovan," the voice repeated.

"Oh. Charlie. It's you. I thought . . ."

"No, guy, it's just me." Ellis perched on the side of Donovan's bunk. "Thought you might want to know that your girlfriend has left camp."

"Who?" He knew who Charlie had to mean by that, of course. But he didn't want to admit that he knew.

"That laundress that's sweet on you, of course. Jeez, John, how many lady friends you got around here, anyway?" Ellis winked. "Must be a lot about you that the rest of us don't know. Anyway, you know that train of emigrants that stopped here last night? Well, she left with them this morning. The way I hear it, she had a hell of a row with Mr. Erickson about money she had coming." He laughed. "She like to tore the store up before he gave in and paid her something. An' then, according to this infantry rube that was in the place at the time, she spit on the floor and cussed Erickson something awful on her way out. Guy said she could cuss better than a top sergeant. Make a mule blush, he claimed."

Charlie shook his head sadly. "I tell you, John, I'm gonna miss that old gal. She didn't look like much, but she could sure give a man a wild ride." He laughed again. "But then, you already know that, don't you."

Donovan was careful to show none of it on his face,

but he felt a hollowness in his stomach in response to Ellis's unknowing comments. It was hard enough knowing that Sarah had taken his advice to leave. He would miss her. But it was even harder for him to think about the implications of the rest of what Charlie said.

"Donovan."

"Yes, Sergeant-Major?"

"Private communication with civilians is not authorized in this man's army."

Donovan had no idea what the man was talking about. "Yes, Sergeant-Major."

"You will destroy this envelope immediately. You will not open it. You will not examine the contents."

"Yes, Sergeant-Major."

He understood then. And this was but another form of deliberate harassment. The sergeant-major wanted to tighten the screws another turn.

Well, it wasn't going to work. None of their nonsense was going to work, damn them.

The sergeant-major handed over a small, none-too-clean envelope with the words "Tpr. John Donovan, 4 Sqd, N Trp" written in a handwriting he'd never seen before. Not that he needed a signature to know who had written it.

"Permission to use the lamp flame, Sergeant-Major?"

"All right, Donovan."

He carefully removed the globe of the oil lamp that was burning inside the orderly room and touched one tip of the envelope to the fire. The envelope and the note it surely contained burned quickly. Donovan held on to a corner of the paper as long as he could before he dropped the still-burning remnant, leaving nothing behind but ash and a very small flake of white paper.

So much for any accusations that he intended to reassemble torn-up scraps and read the contraband note.

They weren't going to get him for a violation of orders that easily, damn them.

He braced himself stiffly to attention. "Is there anything else, Sergeant-Major?"

"No, Donovan. You're dismissed."

"Thank you, Sergeant-Major." He executed an about-face and marched stiffly out of the troop headquarters building.

No, sir. They weren't going to get him that easily. Weren't going to bother him with their foolishness, either. He didn't have to know what was in the note. It was enough for him to know that Sarah cared enough to leave it.

Chapter Sixty

"Jeez, John, I think you're winning. You're actually going on patrol with us instead of staying back for those shitty work details," Sims said.

"Naw," Donovan told him. "They've just run out of lousy stuff for me to do. They'll think up some more goodies while we're out and have them all waiting for me when we get back."

"You ought to go over the hill. You know that, don't you?"

"What? And let them beat me? That'll be the damn day." He stomped his feet to make sure they were comfortably settled into his boots and reached into the sling beneath his bunk—"possum bellies," they were called— for the Spencer. The carbine felt solid and heavy in his hands. And a little unnatural. He'd hardly touched the weapon in almost two months.

"You do what you think best, John, but the guys won't

hold it against you if you want to walk away. A lot of fellows have, and with less reason."

"I know that."

"You ought to think about it anyway."

Donovan laughed. "Me, I get in trouble whenever I try and think. You know?"

"You and me both, buddy."

"You ready, Ed?"

"Sure. Let's go out and make the world safe for movers and emigrants and other damn fools, eh?"

They picked up the rolls of personal gear that would be lashed behind the saddles, checked to make sure their ammunition boxes were heavy with the weight of fresh cartridges, and headed off toward the stables.

The patrol made a brave sight as it climbed into the slanting early-morning sun. They were two days out on an eight-day patrol, roving north and east from Camp Horan, three squads led by Lieutenant Harmon, Four Squad in its now customary place at the rear and with Sims and Donovan acting—also customary this entire time out—acting as dust catchers at the tail end of the procession.

It really was pretty though, Donovan reflected. The golden light of the new day picked out the red and white guidon snapping and fluttering in a fresh breeze, and starbursts of light reflected boldly off the brass and steel accoutrements of the moving column.

It occurred to Donovan that he was intensely proud to be a part of this group of men and never mind the troubles he'd had. The men were staunch and cheerful, solid in a fight with the Indians. Or in slightly less bloody conflict with the infantry.

He'd made friends here. He hadn't expected to.

All he'd wanted when he came here was a refuge from what he left behind. He'd found considerably more.

The lieutenant and Tom Albrecht his guidon bearer neared the crest of a steep rise and rose in their stirrups. At the rear of the column, Donovan was a long way from being able to see what was ahead, but he knew something was afoot. The impression was confirmed when the lieutenant drew his sword—Harmon was the only officer who ever wore one—and turned in his saddle.

There was no bugler with them, so the self-important Harmon had to settle for voice commands. "Patrol. At the trot, ho."

A moment later, the order "At the gallop" was given.

And before Donovan and Sims cleared the ridge, they heard Harmon bawl, "Charge."

Damn fool hadn't remembered to swing the squads onto a wide line, Donovan thought even as he bumped his horse with a spur. They were still in column and had no business charging anything or anybody like that.

They raced over the top of the hill to find Lieutenant Harmon larruping as hard and fast as he could manage down onto a handful of Indian lodges.

The rest of the boys were doing their best to keep up but weren't much serious about it. After all, their carbines were still slung and nobody at either end of the scuffle was offering any sort of a fight.

They could see a few Indians standing around among the tipis, but none of them was armed.

For that matter, none of them seemed particularly excited by the fact that they were the object of a cavalry charge, never mind that it was a small one.

The extent of their excitement was that a couple of

them—old men, both proved to be—stood up and walked toward the near edge of the village.

A dozen or so yellow and red and brindle mutts set up something of a racket. But by then Donovan was pretty sure the Indians knew there was company in the vicinity anyway.

A few women stuck their heads out of tent flaps to see what was going on, then disappeared again with no indications of panic.

The lieutenant actually looked disappointed when he turned in his saddle to face the onrushing men and called for them to quit the charge and return to an orderly formation.

Donovan figured that was that, except the lieutenant's horse chose that particular moment to step in a badger hole and do a somersault with Harmon still in the saddle.

It was awfully hard for Donovan to keep from laughing.

Chapter Sixty-one

They had time to build fires and boil coffee before the lieutenant had wits enough about him to figure out what day of the week it was.

Whatever day that happened to be. It occurred to Donovan that he himself had no notion as to day and date. He'd lost track sometime during the past few months.

In any event, Lieutenant Harmon had an egg on his head big enough to fry up and feed three hungry men, and he needed some time to get back all the air he'd had squished out of him when that horse rolled over him.

Bad off as the lieutenant was, though, the horse was the one that got the worst of the thing. It had a broken leg. Corporal Nesbitt of Two Squad put it down with a Spencer ball behind the ear, and Rathburn made some lifelong friends—or so one would think by the reactions—when he indicated to the old men who were observing all this that the Indians could have the dead horse for lunch.

The Indians hadn't been all that much excited by Lieutenant Harmon's charge, but they surely did react to the prospect of fresh meat. A score or more of exceptionally ugly women came on the run, with knives and baskets at the ready, as quickly as that word went out. Their charge put Harmon's to shame.

By the time the lieutenant had his wits back—such as he'd possessed to start with, anyway—there wasn't much more left of his horse than a big patch of spilt blood and a mound of dung. The intestines that had held the dung were long since divided up, emptied and carried away. Donovan had no idea what the Indians intended doing with the offal and other waste, but they'd wanted most every scrap of it.

Once Harmon was on his feet again, Nesbitt and Rathburn passed the word for the fires to be doused and coffee cups put away.

"Donovan."

"Yes, Corporal?"

"The lieutenant needs a horse. He'll ride yours."

Naturally! He damn near said it aloud, but stopped himself in time. "Yes, Corporal."

"Strip your gear off it."

"Yes, Corporal." He got a perverse sort of pleasure in knowing that it wouldn't be good old Handsome that the lieutenant was taking. Handsome was still in the remount herd. When Donovan returned to duty, he'd been assigned a different horse. He didn't know it for sure, but he suspected Handsome was held back from him deliberately because they knew he liked the ugly old creature. This new mount he hadn't named or yet gotten to know, so it did not bother him to have to be turning it over to the lieutenant now.

Then another thought struck him.

"Corporal."

"Yes, Donovan?"

"If the lieutenant will be riding this horse . . . and his is dead . . ."

"Your orders are to make your way back to the post on your own, Donovan."

"But . . ." He looked rather apprehensively in the direction of the Indian camp.

The small band hadn't seemed threatening, but . . . he did not at all relish the thought that he would be left afoot in plain sight of them, either. And with half a day of sunlight left in which they could ride him down and murder him if they damned well wanted to. Once the patrol moved out of sight, there would only be Donovan and his carbine to stop the Indians from doing anything they wished.

He remembered all too well what had happened to Louie Gordon when he was abandoned on the empty Kansas prairie.

"Jesus!" he blurted.

Chapter Sixty-two

"Donovan."

"Yes, sir?"

"When we get back to the post, I intend to have the sergeant-major personally inspect your equipment. If you've thrown anything away, you will not only pay for it, I will have you stand before a court-martial on charges of willful destruction of government property. Am I clear about that, Donovan?"

"Yes, Lieutenant."

"Very well, then. Carry on."

Donovan wasn't sure if he was supposed to salute the son of a bitch now or not. In all the time he'd been in the army, he'd scarcely had any personal contact with an officer before. Lowly troopers and private soldiers dealt with noncoms, not officers. Still, there didn't seem any harm in saluting, and there certainly could be charges leveled if he failed to salute when he was supposed to.

It took him a moment to remember how he was supposed to manage a salute when he was carrying a carbine. And another moment to dump his saddle and bridle and bedroll on the ground.

By then the lieutenant had turned his horse—Donovan's of late—and was riding stiffly away.

The heck with him. Donovan hadn't wanted to salute him anyway.

"Patrol. At the walk. Forward . . . ho!"

The lieutenant didn't care, but the boys did. The column of twos turned briefly into a file, and the orderly line of march bowed and curved as one by one the boys of One and Four Squads swung by to offer a wave, a wink, or a hasty handshake.

They'd already been by, nearly all of them, to offer advice, encouragement, and bits out of their own supply of rations. Just in case. Several had even offered ammunition.

If Donovan had accepted all of it he wouldn't have been able to carry it, short of buying a mule from the Indians.

Come to think of it, dammit, why hadn't they even tried to buy a horse from the Indians? Not that the ponies were much account. But one of them would have carried him safely along with the patrol or back to Camp Horan or . . . well, an Indian pony would sure be better than being left alone and afoot out here.

But the lieutenant hadn't wanted to do that.

They would break him, Sarah warned. Or kill him, one or the other.

The hell with them. They couldn't break him, and he intended to see to it that they didn't manage to kill him, either. The hell with them, one and all.

He stood, chin high and defiant, as the lieutenant led his patrol off toward the north.

241

Rathburn, the last man Donovan would have expected to bother speaking to him, dropped completely out of the column and waited until even Ed Sims and Trooper John Smith were out of hearing before he approached.

Standing on the ground and looking up at the mounted corporal, Donovan felt small and weak and acutely alone.

"You know your way back, don't you?"

"Yes, Corporal."

"Don't forget what the lieutenant told you. You could be facing a court-martial when you get back."

"I heard him."

"And mind you don't show yourself in the open. Get the hell away from this bunch," he nodded in the direction of the Indians, who were happily feasting on fresh horse meat, "and do your moving at night. There won't be any Injuns about in the night, more'n likely."

"Yes, Corporal."

"Another thing, Donovan. You be careful. It wouldn't do for you to get caught and killed out here. Who knows? If that was to happen, we might never find your body. Men disappear out here all the time. You know that."

He knew it. They all did. Two weeks back, a patrol by One and Three Squads came across part of a skeleton half buried in the mud beside some no-name creek. The man—or, for that matter, maybe it'd been a woman—must have been dead an awfully long time. Most of the bones had been washed away some time in the past, and there was no clothing found. Just the bones and part of a broken knife blade.

They'd had no idea if the dead person was white or Indian, who it was, or how they'd died. Death could happen in the empty places, and no one would ever be the wiser.

242

"If you don't make it back, Donovan, we'll have to put you on the books as missing and presumed dead. Figure these here Injuns got you or their cousins did." Rathburn nodded toward the elderly Cheyenne who had been ignoring the patrol once they had their meat in hand.

"Do you take my meaning, Donovan?"

"I . . . think I do, Corporal."

"Right, then." Rathburn reined his horse away. Then stopped. Without looking back again, he said, "You weren't all that bad a trooper, Donovan."

"Thank you, Corporal. I . . . I'd say you haven't been all that bad a squad leader, neither." The funny thing was, now that he'd said it he decided that it was true.

Rathburn grunted and spurred his mount into a canter to catch up with the rest of the patrol.

Chapter Sixty-three

Rathburn couldn't have made it much plainer. Not unless he'd come right out and ordered Donovan to go over the hill, and he couldn't hardly do that.

Lordy, this wasn't the way he'd intended things to be, though. Not by a long shot.

Not that a man always manages the things he intends. Man proposes and . . . There was a saying about that. Donovan couldn't remember how it went. He had in mind the meaning of it, though. He surely did that.

He sighed and sat down on the issue saddle for a moment to collect his thoughts.

The wind shifted, and he could smell the smoke from the Indians' dung fires and the accompanying scent of roasting horse meat. The lieutenant's horse smelled pretty good, actually.

Rathburn's advice was good. He could get clear of this

village—hopefully; he hadn't seen weapons enough here to challenge his Spencer—then travel by night.

That was what probably did Louie in. He'd found the road and that was fine, but he'd walked it in daylight. Donovan wouldn't make that mistake. He would do all his walking in the night when the Indians wouldn't be watching and couldn't see much if they were looking.

Right now he was . . . he tried to work it out in his mind, although he'd never seen a map of this country . . . right now he ought to be east and somewhat north from Camp Horan.

So if he walked straight west for, say, three days or maybe four, it should be safe enough then for him to turn south again and pick up the wagon road. He wanted to make sure he was west of Horan when he got onto the road.

But still east of Howland's Station. He wanted to stop in there. Just briefly and then he could go on.

He had nearly twenty dollars in his pocket, and a Spencer carbine that ought to be worth something.

That wasn't a bad start for a man.

Or for a man and a woman.

He wondered if . . .

He'd ask. Dammit, he'd ask. He'd said himself that out here a person was who and what they claimed. And how they acted.

There wasn't any reason why man, woman, or both couldn't use that to make a fresh start for themselves.

For a kid, too. That would be only fair.

But first, well, they said there was opportunity aplenty for a man or a woman in the gold camps of Colorado Territory.

He—they—could get there. Somehow. Walk if they

had to. Plenty did. And most of them passed clean across the country without ever seeing a hostile Indian. That's what they said.

Donovan looked at the Indian village, and his mouth ran with the scent coming off those fires.

He thought about the saddle he was sitting on. He'd sure be court-martialed if he showed up at Horan without it. Yessir, Lieutenant Boyd Harmon himself said that.

On the other hand, it just could be that those Cheyenne would want to swap a chunk of fresh-cooked horse meat for a bridle and an army saddle.

Donovan grinned and got to his feet.

He picked up the useless McClellan and carried it over to one of the Indians, an old man who Donovan was pretty sure he'd heard use a few words of English.

A man can walk better, after all, if he has meat in his belly and not so heavy a load to carry.

With a light load and a little determination, why, there's no telling how far a man's feet can carry him.

Maybe even all the way to a good life.

WILL HENRY
THE BEAR PAW HORSES

THE BLAZING SAGA OF ONE MAN'S BATTLE TO SAVE THE SIOUX NATION—AND TO WIN A FIERY REBEL!

Con Jenkins is a horse-thieving murderer who can charm a whiskey drummer out of his sample case or a schoolmarm out of her virtue. With his razor-sharp mind and lightning quick draw, he has carved a reputation for himself from Hole-in-the-Wall to Robber's Roost. So why is Jenkins helping an ancient Indian and his white-hating granddaughter carry out the last orders of Crazy Horse, the most-feared war chief of all the Oglala Sioux? And why is he so determined to save the old medicine man from harm?

Before he can answer those questions, Con Jenkins is thrown headfirst into the deadliest struggle of his life—a battle for the very horses that will bring the Sioux—or the white settlers—their greatest victory.

_4055-7 $4.99 US/$5.99 CAN

WILL HENRY
SAN JUAN HILL

Bestselling Author of *Death of a Legend*

The year is 1898 and Fate Baylen of Arizona's Bell Rock Ranch joins the cavalry to fight the Spanish. But it looks as if the conflict is turning into a haven for graft grabbers, a heyday for incompetent officers, and a holiday for Fates and other boys from the West. Then the fighting starts, and men sweat, curse, turn cowardly, become heroes—and even die. Under the command of the valiant Teddy Roosevelt, Fate musters all the courage he can. Yet as he and the Rough Riders head into battle after battle, Fate can only wonder how many of them will survive to share in the victorious drive to the top of San Juan Hill.

_4045-X $4.99 US/$6.99 CAN

CUSTER

Will Henry

Hated by the Indians, feared by his own men, George Armstrong Custer will stop at nothing in his quest for personal glory. But the daring leader of the illustrious 7th Cavalry will find his most lasting fame in his final defeat—the Indians' greatest victory—at the Little Big Horn. Now, combined for the first time in a single volume, here are Will Henry's two novels of Custer's life: *Yellow Hair,* the story of Custer as a brash, young General; and *Custer's Last Stand,* the tale of his tragic fate. In these classic novels, the West's most legendary figure is brought to life by its finest storyteller.

___4569-9 $5.50 US/$6.50 CAN

Dorchester Publishing Co., Inc.
P.O. Box 6640
Wayne, PA 19087-8640

Please add $1.75 for shipping and handling for the first book and $.50 for each book thereafter. NY, NYC, and PA residents, please add appropriate sales tax. No cash, stamps, or C.O.D.s. All orders shipped within 6 weeks via postal service book rate. Canadian orders require $2.00 extra postage and must be paid in U.S. dollars through a U.S. banking facility.

Name_____
Address_____
City_____ State_____ Zip_____
I have enclosed $_____ in payment for the checked book(s).
Payment <u>must</u> accompany all orders. ❏ Please send a free catalog.
        CHECK OUT OUR WEBSITE! www.dorchesterpub.com

WILDERNESS

TRAPPER'S BLOOD/ MOUNTAIN CAT

DAVID THOMPSON

Trapper's Blood. In the wild Rockies, a man has to act as judge, jury, and executioner against his enemies. And when trappers start turning up dead, their bodies horribly mutilated, Nate King and his friends vow to hunt down the ruthless killers. But taking the law into their own hands, they soon find out that a hasty decision can make them as guilty as the murderers they want to stop.

And in the same action-packed volume...

Mountain Cat. A seasoned hunter and trapper, Nate King can fend off attacks from brutal warriors and furious grizzlies alike. But a hunt for a mountain lion twice the size of other deadly cats proves to be his greatest challenge. If Nate can't destroy the monstrous creature, it will slaughter innocent settlers—and the massacre might well begin with Nate's own family!

___4621-0 $4.99 US/$5.99 CAN

Dorchester Publishing Co., Inc.
P.O. Box 6640
Wayne, PA 19087-8640

Please add $1.75 for shipping and handling for the first book and $.50 for each book thereafter. NY, NYC, and PA residents, please add appropriate sales tax. No cash, stamps, or C.O.D.s. All orders shipped within 6 weeks via postal service book rate. Canadian orders require $2.00 extra postage and must be paid in U.S. dollars through a U.S. banking facility.

Name_____
Address_____
City_____State_____Zip_____
I have enclosed $_____ in payment for the checked book(s).
Payment <u>must</u> accompany all orders. ❑ Please send a free catalog.
  CHECK OUT OUR WEBSITE! www.dorchesterpub.com

LAST OF THE DUANES

Buck Duane's father was a gunfighter who died by the gun, and, in accepting a drunken bully's challenge, Duane finds himself forced into the life of an outlaw. He roams the dark trails of southwestern Texas, living in outlaw camps, until he meets the one woman who can help him overcome his past—a girl named Jennie Lee.

___4430-7 $4.99 US/$5.99 CAN

Dorchester Publishing Co., Inc.
P.O. Box 6640
Wayne, PA 19087-8640

Please add $1.75 for shipping and handling for the first book and $.50 for each book thereafter. NY, NYC, and PA residents, please add appropriate sales tax. No cash, stamps, or C.O.D.s. All orders shipped within 6 weeks via postal service book rate. Canadian orders require $2.00 extra postage and must be paid in U.S. dollars through a U.S. banking facility.

Name_____
Address_____
City_____State_____Zip_____
I have enclosed $_____ in payment for the checked book(s).
Payment <u>must</u> accompany all orders. ☐ Please send a free catalog.
CHECK OUT OUR WEBSITE! www.dorchesterpub.com

ZANE GREY

RANGERS OF THE LONE STAR

Deputy Marshal Russ Sittell is on special assignment from the Texas Rangers to work with Vaughan Steele in putting a stop to the rampant rustling in Pecos County. But everyone knows that local rancher—and mayor—Granger Longstreth doesn't want any Ranger interference in his town. When Russ takes a job on Longstreth's ranch, he's able to learn exactly how the rancher operates—and he witnesses the growing tension between Longstreth and Steele. A tension that can lead only to trouble.

___4556-7 $4.99 US/$5.99 CAN

Dorchester Publishing Co., Inc.
P.O. Box 6640
Wayne, PA 19087-8640

Please add $1.75 for shipping and handling for the first book and $.50 for each book thereafter. NY, NYC, and PA residents, please add appropriate sales tax. No cash, stamps, or C.O.D.s. All orders shipped within 6 weeks via postal service book rate. Canadian orders require $2.00 extra postage and must be paid in U.S. dollars through a U.S. banking facility.

Name_____
Address_____
City_____ State_____ Zip_____
I have enclosed $_____ in payment for the checked book(s).
Payment <u>must</u> accompany all orders. ❏ Please send a free catalog.
    CHECK OUT OUR WEBSITE! www.dorchesterpub.com